# THE PINK HOUSE

CINDY KIRK

WAVERLY
HOUSE

ISBN: 9798840486719

# CHAPTER ONE

"Pack it, or smash it?" Standing in the middle of a room full of boxes, Hannah Danbury lifted one hand palm up then the other as she weighed the options.

Her BFF, Emma Sands, held the mug sporting the logo of Hannah's former employer between two fingers, a look of distaste on her face. "I vote smash it."

Though tempted, Hannah shook her head. "If I did smash it, I'd be the one cleaning up the mess. Not worth it."

"Please don't tell me you're going to keep it. Not after what they did to you."

Hannah hesitated for only an instant. "It's a good mug, but not for me. Put it in the donate pile."

Emma offered a reluctant nod as Hannah continued to drop utensils into a box labeled Kitchen Stuff.

"You gave that company over eight years of your life." Emma's lips pursed. "Don't tell me they couldn't have found a place for you when they restructured."

The thought had crossed Hannah's mind a dozen times, but ruminating on her dismissal served no purpose. She hadn't been the only one let go when the company had been sold. A lot of really good employees had found themselves without jobs.

"Layoffs happen." That was Hannah's go-to phrase whenever anyone had expressed sympathy during the past eight weeks. "Restructuring is part of corporate life nowadays."

"True, but they don't usually happen when you're still grieving for…" Her voice trailed off, and sympathy filled Emma's brown eyes.

"Brian. You can say his name, Ems. I don't forget he's gone just because we don't talk about him." Last year, Hannah's formerly healthy husband had been diagnosed with cancer only months before his thirtieth birthday. He'd died six weeks later. "Brian is always with me. I look around this apartment and see him everywhere. It breaks my heart to think of all the dreams we had—he had—that will never come true."

"Let's take a break." Emma set the mug on the island counter and gestured toward the sofa. "Is that the real reason you're leaving Greensboro? To get away from the memories?"

Hannah stepped around several boxes to drop onto the sofa. She had asked herself the same question Emma was asking.

"If I was still employed at Mingus, I'd stay. With no income and my dad's house in GraceTown falling into my lap…" Hannah shrugged. "Seems like the perfect time to return home."

"I'm happy for you, I really am, but I'm sad for me. I wish home wasn't Maryland." Emma grabbed two sodas from the refrigerator. After handing one can to Hannah, she took a seat beside her friend on the sofa. "I mean, GraceTown is adorable, but it's not like it's down the block."

Hannah reached over and gave her friend's hand a squeeze. "I'm going to miss you, too. Big-time."

They sipped their sodas in companionable silence before Emma shifted to face Hannah. "I've never asked. I mean, I know your dad won't be there, but what about Brian's parents? Do they still live in GraceTown?"

Hannah nodded. "They do, but I doubt I'll see much of them. Brian's sister, Katie, and her new husband are in town, and Katie and her mom are close."

Hannah had liked her in-laws well enough. With her own mother passing away when she was small, she'd hoped to forge a closeness with Debbie. That connection had never materialized.

"In a way, with your dad and stepmom already in Florida, it's like you're moving to a completely new town."

"I suppose." Hannah lifted the can of soda, but didn't take a drink. "Except I did grow up there."

Emma pushed silky brown hair back from her heart-shaped face with the back of her hand, the gesture as elegant as the woman herself. "Are you going to look for another marketing position once you get settled?"

This wasn't the first time Emma had broached the topic of Hannah resuming her career. Like Hannah had once been, Emma was all about opportunities and advancement. Each time before when Emma had asked, Hannah had simply told her the truth—she wasn't sure what she would do.

Since she knew Emma worried, Hannah brought up a possibility that had recently surfaced, one she found intriguing. "Mackenna, she's a friend from way back, works at Collister College. We've stayed in touch through the years, mostly online. She mentioned they have a position in marketing and student recruitment coming open in September. She thinks I'd be a fabulous candidate and offered to put in a good word."

"September is four months away." Emma lowered her soda. "Do you really want to wait that long? Plus, there's no guarantee you'd get the job."

"I know that." Hannah kept her tone matter-of-fact. "But it sounds as if it could be a possibility."

In fact, it was the first position that had interested her, though she was sure the appeal was because she'd be working in the same area as Mackenna.

Thankfully, she had time to consider all her options. Brian had carried a robust life insurance policy, and Hannah had yet to touch any of the money. Between it and what she was making off the sale of the townhouse, she could easily take the summer off.

She told herself she deserved the break. It had been a tough year, with the past couple of months being the roughest. She'd lost her job, learned her dad was leaving GraceTown for sunny Florida, then she'd decided to put her own home on the market and move. The hits just kept coming with the first anniversary of Brian's death last week, six days before their thirtieth birthday.

When she and Brian had first started dating, sharing a birthday had seemed incredibly cool. Now that day would forever be a yearly reminder of all she'd lost.

"We thought we had all the time in the world." Hannah gazed out the window. "We had a plan. Our twenties would be focused on building our careers. The thirties, well, that was when we planned to start a family. Now here I am, turning thirty and making new plans alone."

"Speaking of birthdays." Emma placed a hand on Hannah's arm and gave it a sympathetic squeeze before rising. Hurrying across the room, she stopped where she'd dropped her stuff when she arrived. She returned to the sofa with a white bakery box.

Emma's eyes met hers. "I know you said you didn't want to go out and celebrate. But we're not going out, we're here."

A smile tugged at the corners of Hannah's lips. "What do you have in there?"

"It struck me that this could be the last time we'll be able to celebrate your birthday together." Carefully opening the bakery box, Emma removed a cupcake. "I say a birthday without cake is like sex without a man."

With its swirl of pink frosting dotted with tiny beads of white that resembled pearls and topped with a pink crown, the cupcake reminded Hannah of something out of a fairy tale.

A pretty bow of organza ribbon edged with pink satin encircled the base. Emma held out the gorgeous creation. "A cupcake worthy of a princess for a princess."

A lump formed in Hannah's throat. "It-it's gorgeous."

"It's from that new bakery out on Whittier." Emma pushed the cupcake at her when Hannah only stared. "The reviews say their cupcakes taste every bit as good as they look."

"Thank you, Ems." Tears stung the backs of Hannah's eyes at her friend's thoughtfulness. "You're going to have to help me eat it."

"No way am I making you share. Not on your birthday." Emma smiled and pulled another cupcake from the box. "That's why I got one for myself."

The laughter that bubbled up in Hannah was as precious a gift as the gorgeous cupcake and the beautiful friend beside her.

∼

Three weeks later, Hannah moved into the only home she'd known before leaving for college at eighteen.

Though the house hadn't changed, GraceTown had continued to grow and now spread in all directions. Homes dotted ground where crops had once flourished.

Like the hardworking people who inhabited these homes, the houses in Hannah's neighborhood remained untouched by the passage of time. In the block she considered her own, the homes were older and boasted two stories and large front porches. Blankets of lush green grass and flowering bushes spoke to the pride of ownership.

Many of the neighbors were the same. Sean O'Malley from down the street had a ladder resting against the trunk of a large pin oak as he sawed off a limb.

Geraldine Walker and Beverly Raymond still lived across the street.

In their early seventies, with hair now sporting more gray

than brown, the two women waved from their porch swing as she drove by.

As Hannah waved back and called out a greeting through her open car window, she realized just how much she was looking forward to living in a neighborhood again.

The townhouse she and Brian had purchased right after college had been located in an area of Greensboro, North Carolina, called Friendly West. They'd been happy in the area inhabited by mostly young professionals, men and women focused on their careers and more interested in their own personal activities than socializing with neighbors.

She understood the focus. She and Brian had embraced that same lifestyle, working long hours, then filling any free hours with time spent together.

Hannah hoped to do things differently this time. While she would always give a job her best, never again would she let a career consume her life.

Though she'd meant what she'd said to Emma about understanding that layoffs happen, it still hurt to be cast aside after eight years of unwavering loyalty.

Hannah shoved the thought aside. She would not bring old regrets into her new life.

After setting a box of kitchen items on the counter, Hannah returned to her vehicle. Thankfully, her father had left most of his furniture, which had saved her the cost of moving hers.

Though she had to admit that parting with the sofa, chairs and bedroom furniture she and Brian had chosen together had been more difficult than she'd imagined.

Each piece had been purchased after much consideration and debate. She remembered one spirited discussion that had ended with them making love on the floor where their new sofa would eventually sit. Afterward, relaxed and sated, they'd come to a meeting of the minds on fabric.

Hannah's hand stilled on a box of dishes, the memory bittersweet. Brian had been so healthy, so fit, so incredibly vibrant and alive…until he wasn't.

"Need help?"

The unexpected voice had Hannah whirling, nearly hitting her head on the side of the hatch of her car. She blinked and realized this was no stranger offering assistance. This man was someone she knew. "Charlie?"

"Hey, you remember." He flashed an easy grin that was as much a part of him as the worn jeans and the dark wavy hair that went past his collar.

"How could I forget?" Her tone turned droll. "You were in our wedding."

Not just *in* the wedding. He'd been Brian's best man. Their friendship had been one Hannah had never understood.

While her husband and Charlie had both been popular athletes and good-looking guys in high school, Charlie had struck her as over-the-top loud and something of a show-off.

Brian had always told her that if she took the time to get to know Charlie, she'd like him. There had never been an opportunity. The two boys had gone to different colleges, and after graduation, she and Brian had married and settled in Greensboro.

"I'm sorry I couldn't make the funeral." Charlie shifted from one foot to the other. "My mom was in the hospital and pretty sick. With my dad out of the picture, I needed to stay close."

"I understand." Those days were a blur anyway. Besides, Charlie had always struck her as a wildcard, and she hadn't needed any drama at the service. There had been enough with Brian's mother fainting and hitting her head, necessitating a 911 call.

Hannah remembered wishing she could just give in to her grief, weep uncontrollably and fall apart, leaving someone else to pick up the pieces.

Instead, she'd gone on autopilot and made the arrangements,

contacted everyone who needed to be reached and comforted Brian's parents.

Only in her townhouse, once everyone had left and all the duties were done, had it hit her. Brian, with his laughing hazel eyes and bright smile, would never again kiss her, hold her or call her Hannah Banana. All the dreams she'd had for the future had died with him.

"Hannah." Charlie's tone gentled. "You okay?"

How many times during the past year had she been asked that same question? Fifty? A hundred?

She'd discovered there was only one suitable answer, preferably accompanied by a slight smile.

"I'm fine." Taking in a breath, she expelled it slowly. "Or I will be once I get all this stuff unloaded and inside."

"I'll help." Charlie didn't wait for a response. He simply scooped up a box containing wedding china and hefted it as easily as if it held feathers.

"Thanks." Hannah grabbed a box of her own and followed him into the house.

"Where do you want this?" he asked.

For a second, she considered telling him to just set it down in the living room, but she knew she'd have to eventually move it. "Would you mind putting it on the dining room table?"

"No problem." He set the box on a table that sported a thin layer of dust.

Hannah stood there for a moment, studying the mahogany table and matching china hutch, relics of a bygone era. She'd want to update, that much was certain. But until she had a clear vision of how she wanted to update the interior, she'd put what was here to good use.

"Your father thought about taking these pieces with him to Florida, but Sandie was having none of it."

Sandie, whom her father had married last year, had very definite ideas. Her dad appeared to take the woman's bossiness in stride. Hannah figured he must see something in her. After nearly thirty years as a widower, he'd finally taken the plunge.

"In this instance, I agree with Sandie. Leaving them behind made sense. The pieces are heavy and would have cost a fortune to move." Hannah shook her head. "Plus, I've seen pictures of their Florida home. These wouldn't fit in at all."

"Your dad still had a hard time walking away." Charlie's sharp-eyed gaze surveyed the dated decor. "He told me it felt like he was leaving a part of himself behind."

Hannah understood. She'd felt the same about her furniture in Greensboro.

"What else did my dad tell you?" Hannah hadn't even known that Charlie and her father were that well acquainted.

"That knowing you'd be living here was a comfort."

Now, this was getting weird. Hannah lifted a hand. "Tell me again how you know my father."

Surprise skittered across Charlie's face. "Neighbors talk."

"Neighbors? You don't live around here." Hannah struggled to recall just where Charlie lived, then decided the mental gymnastics weren't worth the effort. That had been high school. Undoubtedly, he'd moved numerous times since then.

"My mom and I live next door." He jerked his head toward the north. "We moved in last year."

"You live with your mother?"

Charlie arched a dark brow. "You have a problem with that?"

"Nope." Hannah wasn't surprised, not really. Just like she hadn't been surprised when Brian had told her that Charlie had dropped out of the engineering program at MIT after two years. Brian said it was because Charlie was so smart he was bored. Hannah suspected too much partying. "Listen, you don't have to help me."

He grinned. "What box do you want brought in next?"

With Charlie's help, they emptied the back of her car in short order.

As she watched him carry box after box, Hannah had to admit that Charlie had retained his youthful good looks. His hair was still glossy, thick and dark and his body as muscular and lean as it had been during his football days.

Either he worked out regularly, or his day job involved a lot of lifting, because he had no problem handling any of the boxes, even ones she'd overfilled.

"That's the last." He set the box where she'd instructed in the main-floor bedroom. "Anything else I can help with?"

"No, thank you." This time, Hannah's smile came easy. "You've been very helpful."

"Brian was my friend. You're my neighbor." He cleared his throat. "If you ever need anything—"

He lifted a marker from the table and wrote a phone number on the top of the nearest box. "Call anytime, or stop over. I'm right next door."

With a wink, he turned and strode out the door.

Hannah glanced at the number, but made no move to add it to her phone. Instead, she began unpacking, determined to put the past behind her and start a new life.

Without Brian.

# CHAPTER TWO

"I'm going to bake some cookies for Hannah," Lisa told her son over dinner. "I think it'd be a nice way to welcome her back to the neighborhood."

"Your cookies are amazing." Charlie wasn't sure that Hannah was the cookie type. She had the look of someone who preferred protein shakes and salads to sweets. Then again, he could be wrong. Despite her having been married to his best friend, he didn't know Hannah well.

"How did your day go?" His mother inclined her head. She was an attractive woman in her mid-fifties with dark hair and eyes of quiet brown. "Did you unravel the mystery of the design flaw?"

"Not yet." Charlie finished off the last bite of brisket on his plate. It had been his turn to cook this evening, and he had to admit he made a killer brisket. "I'm getting closer."

"You'll figure it out." His mom offered an encouraging smile. "I have faith."

She'd always had faith in him. He couldn't have asked for a better, more supportive mother. There wasn't anything he wouldn't do for her.

would not worry about her dad and Sandie's relationship or about all the work around the house that needed to be done.

Lacing up her boots, Hannah headed out the front door and turned toward the woods.

Taking long, brisk strides, with the sun hot against her face, Hannah quickly crossed the small meadow between her home and the tall trees. She paused briefly to inhale the sweet aroma of wild bergamot and rose mallow.

A smile lifted her lips as she recalled telling Brian that, for their generation, stopping to smell the roses was a myth. No one she knew, not a single person, had time in their busy day to smell flowers.

Now, Hannah found herself wishing she and Brian had taken time to walk hand in hand on sweet-smelling summer evenings, maybe pausing to admire the rapid beats of a hummingbird's wings as it hovered above their butterfly bush. Even if they'd only sat on one of the benches positioned around a nearby pond and talked.

If she could go back, there would be a lot of things she'd change. But, as she'd learned all too well this past year, time marched in only one direction.

The woods looming before her had always been one of her favorite places to explore. Though her father had warned her as a child to not venture in too far, she'd always walked until she found the perfect log or tree root to sit on and read.

With the scents and sounds of the forest surrounding her, Hannah would pull out a book, and the world around her would disappear. Brian had appreciated, but not shared, her love of reading.

He'd preferred a pickup game of basketball at the gym or working on his golf game. There had been time for little else. Certainly not for long walks while holding hands. Work had been his passion and his priority. His phone had always been close, even during his off-hours.

Basketball. Golf. Surely there had been more. During the past twelve months, the memories had faded until they felt almost like a dream.

"I won't forget you, Bri," she murmured. "Not ever."

As she continued deeper into the woods, she wondered if it was like that for her dad. Did he still remember the way her mother had laughed? What had always made her smile? Or had those images dimmed so much over the nearly three decades she'd been gone that only the strongest memories remained?

Hannah had been only two when Charlotte Danbury had passed away. Her mother had developed a UTI. By the time she'd gone to the doctor, she was already septic. Within twenty-four hours, she was dead.

As she'd gotten older, Hannah had asked to see pictures of her mother. The tips of her father's ears had turned red when he'd admitted he'd gone a little crazy when his beloved Charlotte had died.

One night, after too many beers, he'd placed all her pictures in a shoe box and put them in a safe place. He'd hoped that having them out of sight would stop the unrelenting pain. It hadn't, of course.

The next morning, he couldn't recall where he'd hidden them. Over the years, they'd both searched for the box, but had never located it.

For years, Hannah had tried to get her dad to describe her mother for her. All she knew was her mother's hair had been light like hers.

In Hannah's imagination, her mother had kind eyes, like Lisa Rogan, the librarian. Though it seemed like two would be too young to remember anything, Hannah swore she remembered the feel of her mother's arms around her and the sweet scent of lily-of-the-valley perfume.

*Funny how you can miss someone you barely knew.* For her, grief was a gentle yearning that hadn't faded even as the years passed.

She strode deeper into the woods, recalling how her friends in high school had complained about their mothers. Yet, in another breath, they'd spoken of shopping trips, mani-pedis and long conversations with someone who loved them unconditionally.

Hannah had only her father. To his credit, he'd tried to listen and had always done his best to understand her concerns. Still, he was an IT geek, more comfortable with computers than people. His sigh of relief whenever their personal conversations had ended had been audible.

Branches snapped beneath Hannah's boots as she continued on her way to, well, she wasn't quite sure. She only knew she'd recognize the perfect spot when she reached it.

The buzzing of her phone let her know a reminder had popped up. Hannah had promised to meet Mackenna at a street dance tonight. Since she wasn't meeting her until eight, there was no rush. Still, she couldn't linger in the woods for too long.

The repetitive sound of *peter-peter-peter* had Hannah cocking her head. She'd grown up in this area, knew many of the birds by sight and sound, if not by name.

This particular birdsong wasn't familiar. Eager to see the bird, she turned in the direction of the sound, weaving her way around trees and brush and over tree stumps.

Hannah came to an abrupt stop, the bird forgotten. Her breath hitched at the sight of a two-story *pink* house. On three sides of the structure, dozens of lily-of-the-valley plants bloomed.

The flowers might have caught her eye, but it was the massive structure, complete with a cupola, that captivated her. As Hannah stared, she spotted several women sitting around a table, laughing while they played cards.

Hannah wondered how it was she'd never run across this house before. Though in good repair, the structure wasn't new. If she had to guess, she'd say it appeared to have been built in the early twentieth century.

As she watched, one of the women, her hair the color of butterscotch candy, caught sight of her and lifted a hand in a friendly wave.

Hannah waved back and returned the woman's smile. For a brief moment, she considered approaching the house, but she didn't want to intrude on their game.

With a regret she didn't quite understand, Hannah returned the way she'd come.

It took Hannah longer than she'd expected to find her way out of the woods. After several wrong turns, she finally stepped out into the sunshine. Breathing a sigh of relief, she saw her house, a white beacon against the blue of the sky.

After leaving the pink house, Hannah had fought a feeling of loneliness. The feeling was familiar. During her childhood, the same wave of loneliness would often wash over her, even though her father had been home every evening and had slept just down the hall from her.

While her grief after Brian's death had been overwhelming, she hadn't experienced that sense of being alone in the world.

Maybe it was because she'd had a circle of girlfriends in Greensboro who'd rallied around her to provide unwavering support.

Despite the warmth of the sun, Hannah shivered. She paused at the edge of the clearing and rubbed her arms.

How could she have missed seeing the pink house before? Granted, she'd taken a number of turns today, ones she couldn't re-create if she tried, but that didn't explain why she hadn't stumbled across it at some point in the past. And who had the women been on the porch?

Even as she started across the clearing to her home, she was seized with a sudden urge to go back. Only this time, she wouldn't stand back and watch, she'd march up to the porch and introduce herself.

Then she'd have answers to the questions circling in her brain. As tempted as Hannah was to return to the pink house, she'd promised to meet Mackenna, though.

Her trek through the woods had been a dirty one. Which meant, before she headed to the street dance, she needed to make herself presentable.

Learning more about the pink house and the ladies on the porch would have to wait for another day.

# CHAPTER THREE

As she dressed for the GraceTown in the Streets festival, Hannah wondered if she should have asked Mackenna what most women their age would be wearing this evening. Then she reminded herself she'd grown up in this town and had been back here numerous times over the years.

Some things remained constant. Casual was the name of the game for community events. That wasn't to say that people didn't like to get dressed up for symphony events or the big New Year's Eve bash, but for most everything else, comfortable worked.

After having the Uber drop her off just shy of the historic district, Hannah enjoyed the walk down the pedestrian path to where she would meet Mackenna. The music from the band that drifted on the evening air had Hannah's hips swaying as she made her way down the brick walkway.

Vendors had set up on both sides of Cripple Creek. There were several walking bridges over the creek, so those attending the dance could easily go from one side to the other. From the number of pedestrians on the bridge up ahead, that's just what was happening.

Inspired by the River Walk in San Antonio, the parklike area had been under construction for most of Hannah's childhood. There had been lots of celebrating when it reached completion at the beginning of her senior year in high school.

Hannah remembered strolling these walkways when she and Brian had returned to GraceTown as young adults. Though they had attended the same high school, it had been a large school, and she'd known him only by sight and reputation.

He'd been the popular athlete everyone adored. She'd been the bookish honor student with a core group of friends and a limited social life.

Hannah liked to think she'd come into her own during college. She and Brian had connected when they'd both been new students at Chapel Hill. They'd been partners in chem lab and had bonded over the fact they were both from GraceTown.

He'd made plenty of friends by then, and so had she. Being on her own had been a heady experience. While she hadn't gone crazy being out from under her father's thumb, she'd been able to stay out past eleven without getting grounded.

"What brings that smile to your face?"

Hannah turned, and there was Charlie, looking like every woman's fantasy in jeans and a chambray shirt. Every woman but her, she qualified.

Still, the surprise, or perhaps it was the intoxicating scent of his cologne, had her answering without thinking. "I was remembering how, when I went off to college, I could finally stay out past eleven."

Charlie blinked. "Pardon?"

"Eleven was my curfew in high school." Hannah waved an airy hand. "The only time I got to stay out later was once I graduated from high school."

"Seriously?" His brown eyes betrayed his disbelief. "My curfew was two."

Hannah chuckled. "That explains why you had a robust social life, while my best nights were spent with characters in books."

~

The band played until midnight, then, much like Cinderella's coach, they and their instruments disappeared. Since the food trucks and drink vendors were still open, Hannah and her friends stayed. Slowly, they began drifting off, one by one.

"How did you get here?" Mackenna lived downtown in one of the renovated buildings. For her, it was a short walk home.

"I got an Uber." Hannah pulled out her phone. "I knew finding a parking space down here would be crazy."

"Ubers are going to be in short supply right now."

Hannah turned, and there was Charlie. She'd seen him off and on this evening, but other than at the beginning of the festival and for a while when they'd been dancing, their paths hadn't crossed. Which had been fine with her.

This night had been about reconnecting with girlfriends and having fun with them.

"You think getting an Uber will be difficult?" Hannah's finger poised above the app.

"I know it will." His tone remained matter-of-fact. "Grace-Town is seriously understaffed when it comes to any ride-sharing options. Events like these, well, that's when that lack of staffing is most pronounced."

"It's true," Mackenna told her. "Come with me to my place. I'll get my car and take you home."

"Or…" Charlie lifted a hand. "You could ride home with me. I'm headed in your direction anyway."

"That's right." Mackenna flashed a smile. "I'd forgotten you and your mom moved last year."

It appeared that Hannah riding home with Charlie was a done deal. After all, it would be silly to ask Mackenna to drive her when Charlie was already headed in that direction.

Mackenna flung her arms around Hannah and squeezed tight. "I'm so glad you came tonight. We'll talk soon."

"Hey," Charlie protested. "Don't I get a hug and a 'glad you came tonight, Charlie'?"

With a laugh, Mackenna gave Charlie not only a hug, but a big, smacking kiss on the cheek. "I'm glad you came tonight, Charlie."

With a wave, Mackenna hurried to catch up with a couple who'd called out a greeting to her.

Hannah considered her options. She really didn't like being put in a situation that—

"If you'd prefer to call an Uber, I'll wait with you until it arrives."

The offer had her inclining her head.

"It's obvious you're not keen on riding with me. That's cool." He gestured to the thinning crowd. "But it's late. I don't like the idea of you waiting alone for a ride."

"Are you rescinding your ride offer?"

Surprise skittered across his face. "My offer stands."

"Then I accept."

"You were right about close parking places being difficult to find," he told her as they started walking. "My truck is about a mile from here."

She slanted a look in his direction. "I don't mind walking."

They strolled for a couple of blocks in companionable silence before he spoke. "How do you like being back?"

It was a variation of a question she'd been asked all evening, usually accompanied by an expectant smile, as if the person asking waited for her to say it was good to be home, or something to that effect.

"It's strange," she surprised herself by saying.

If he was puzzled by her odd response, it didn't show.

"There's so much that's familiar." Hannah thought of what she'd told Emma before leaving Greensboro. "The streets and a lot of the buildings are the same as when I grew up here. But even this area," Hannah gestured with one hand, "is so different.

And of my close friends, well, Mackenna is the only one who's still single."

"What about me?"

She chuckled. "You and I were never friends."

"We could have been."

She laughed and rolled her eyes. "No. That would never have happened."

Though he smiled, Hannah got the feeling that her words had hurt him, which wasn't what she'd intended.

"That wasn't a slam against you." As soon as she placed a hand on his arm, he came to a stop. She met his gaze. "Back in high school, I wasn't friends with Brian either. You guys ran in a different crowd. Neither of you knew I existed."

The stiff set to his shoulders eased. "You and I had English together senior year."

"We did?" She paused, and then she remembered and smiled. "That's right. You sat in the back with Kenny Dunham. You guys were always laughing about something."

"Don't you mean disrupting the class?"

"That, too."

He shrugged. "English didn't interest me."

"I liked it," Hannah admitted, "but Mrs. Mason wasn't much of a teacher."

"My mom told me later that she and her husband were having issues that year. They eventually got a divorce."

"I guess you never really know what someone is going through."

He nodded. "If there's anything I can do to make your transition easier, I hope you'll let me know."

"Why would you help me?"

"We're neighbors." As if still seeing the skeptical look on her face, he continued. "Brian was my best friend."

Expelling a breath, Hannah nodded.

"This is it." Charlie gestured to a red 4x4 parked at the curb.

open the door, then she blinked. "Oh, I'm sorry. I thought you were Charlie. He's always forgetting his phone."

"Just me. Returning your plate and thanking you for the delicious cookies." Hannah held out the plate with the cupcakes. "I was experimenting with a new recipe. These were made with fresh raspberries and blueberries."

"Sounds yummy." Lisa studied the cupcakes. "They're also gorgeous. What kind of topping is that? I've never seen anything like it."

"Orange-infused buttercream with edible glitter and glitter stars."

"Charlie is going to love these." Lisa gave a little laugh. "Who am I kidding? I can't wait to try one. Please come in."

"Where would you like me to put these?" Hannah wasn't about to force Lisa to deal with the plate, not when she could see her jerky movements.

"On the dining room table would be lovely."

"I hope I'm not interrupting." Through the opening leading into the dining room, Hannah noticed an open laptop and papers nearby.

"Not at all." As if seeing the direction of her gaze, Lisa smiled. "I do some work for Collister College, but what I'm focused on now isn't time-sensitive."

"Please sit." Lisa gestured to the sofa in the living room.

After setting the plate on the table, Hannah took a seat on the sofa.

Lisa eased herself into a nearby chair with a black mesh back.

"What is it you do for Collister?" Hannah asked once Lisa was settled.

"I'm what's called a cataloger. I analyze current metadata standards and look for ways to improve the college's systems. The goal is to make it easier for students and professors to find what they're looking for in the library system." Lisa gave a little laugh. "That's probably more than you wanted to know, but I love it. I'm grateful I found something I can do from home and use my degree. I also do some freelance work for other entities."

"I remember when you worked at our branch library."

Lisa smiled. "I have a master's in library and information science."

"That's impressive."

"I don't know about that, but it's the perfect field for my skill set and interests. I loved being a community librarian, but this is perfect for me now." Lisa inclined her head. "What about you?"

Hannah waited for the question that was certain to follow, the *What are you going to do now that you're in GraceTown?* When it didn't come, Hannah was left to fill the silence. "I worked in marketing in Greensboro for a manufacturing company. I was downsized shortly before I moved here."

"I'm sorry to hear that." Sympathy filled Lisa's voice. "I thought perhaps you were able to work remotely."

"Nope." Hannah attempted to force her lips into the semblance of a smile, but couldn't make it happen. "That job was my first professional position out of college. I liked it, but I didn't love it. Still, getting cut stung."

Lisa's gaze grew thoughtful. "I believe letting go of old dreams is difficult, no matter the circumstances."

"Old dreams?"

"I'm sure when you started there, you had specific plans for how your career and your life would go." Lisa's eyes took on a distant glow. "I know when I started with the GraceTown Library System, I had no plans to leave."

"Why did you?" Then, fearing that had been too personal a question, Hannah raised her hand. "No need to answer if you don't want. I just meant you were so good at what you did."

"Thank you, Hannah. I loved the children and encouraging their interest in reading." Lisa expelled a breath. "When I was first diagnosed with MS, my ability to get around took a hit. Over the years, I've had my ups and downs. With this job, if I'm having a bad day—or week—I don't have to get out."

Hannah glanced at the staircase. "I would think a two-story home would prove difficult."

"My bedroom and bath are on the main floor. Charlie takes care of the upstairs as well as all the maintenance on the home." A soft look filled Lisa's brown eyes. "When his dad left, I was in pretty bad shape physically. And, well, if I'm being honest, emotionally, too. Charlie left college and moved in to help me out. But the house I lived in then didn't have the shop area he needed for his work. He made do. When this home came on the market, it was perfect for both of us."

Hannah still didn't fully understand exactly what it was Charlie did, but now didn't seem the time to ask. "I'm glad it worked out."

"It has."

"I'll let you get back to work, but first, there's something I hope you can help me with."

Lisa's smile came quick and fast. "Absolutely. Whatever I can do."

"When I took a walk in the woods the other day, I ran across a pink house."

"A pink house?" Lisa gestured toward the window. "In our woods?"

Hannah leaned forward, her voice quivering with excitement. "Have you seen it?"

When Lisa began shaking her head, Hannah added, "Or heard of it?"

"I don't do much hiking these days." Lisa offered a rueful smile. "But back when I did, I never saw any house, not even a cabin. I've also not heard anyone mention a pink house. Was it abandoned?"

"No." Hannah brought up the scene in her memory. "It appeared to be in good repair. There were women playing cards and sipping tea on the porch. One of them waved, really friendly-like."

"I wish I could help, but I'm afraid I don't know anything about a house in the woods." Lisa met her gaze. "Have you asked Charlie?"

"I did." Hannah expelled a breath.

"No luck there either?"

Hannah shook her head.

"It's intriguing, though, isn't it?"

Hannah cocked her head.

"Like a secret garden kind of thing."

"There's the booklover in you." Hannah was laughing as the door swung open.

She and Lisa turned as one, and there was Charlie, a grocery bag in each arm.

"Mom, they were out of avocados," he began, then stopped. "Hannah, hello."

Hannah pushed to her feet. "I just stopped over to drop off some cupcakes and return your mother's plate. I should get going."

"Don't rush off on my account."

"I'm not." Hannah turned to Lisa. "I've kept you from your work long enough. I really enjoyed visiting with you and catching up."

Lisa pushed herself awkwardly to her feet, one hand closing around the top of the chair for support. "I've enjoyed it, too. Stop over anytime. I've missed you."

The words had the blood sliding like warm honey through Hannah's veins. Hannah shifted her gaze to Charlie. "Well, good-bye."

"I'll walk you out." Setting the bags on a side table, he cast his mother a warning glance. "Don't touch those sacks. I'll be right back to put them away."

"You can be so bossy." Affection wove like a pretty ribbon through Lisa's words.

"I take after my mother." Charlie shot his mom a wink, then pushed the door open for Hannah and stepped back.

Hannah expected him to let the door shut and return to the groceries. Instead, he followed her off the porch.

Since the windows were open, he waited until they were a distance from the house to speak. "Thanks for coming over. Since we moved, she doesn't get many visitors."

"I like your mother," Hannah said simply. "I always have."

"She's always liked you."

"I asked her about the pink house," she blurted. "She's never seen or heard of it."

"She doesn't get out much—"

"That's what she said." Hannah blew out an exasperated breath. "I tried to find it again, but couldn't."

"I know the feeling."

Hannah arched a brow. "You've been searching for pink houses?"

He laughed. "No, but I know how it feels to be looking for something, to be so close to finding it, but have it just out of reach."

An odd comment, but fearing a question might launch some heavy-duty discussion, Hannah kept her response vague. "It's nice that you can work from home."

At his questioning look, she added, "So that you can be there for your mother."

"She's a good person who's stayed strong despite some tough breaks. I want to do whatever I can to make her life easier." He chuckled. "I never thought I'd be living with my mother when I was thirty, but regardless of what people think or say, the current arrangement works well for both of us."

Hannah recalled her first thoughts when she'd heard Charlie lived with his mother. Shame flooded her.

"It can be difficult when people make assumptions, when they judge." She paused to steady her voice. "I'm trying to do better at that."

Shoving his hands into his pockets, he rocked back on his heels. "Sounds as if you might have been on the receiving end of some of that judgment."

"The minister at Brian's funeral asked my dad if we'd been having marital troubles before Brian died, because I didn't seem to be grieving enough." Hannah gave a humorless chuckle. "He didn't seem to realize that it was taking all my self-control to hold it together so everything could get done."

"Jerk." Charlie spat the word. "He had no right saying something like that."

"No, he didn't. Just like those who judge your arrangement with your mother have no right."

He nodded. Grinned. "I knew there was a tie-in somewhere. I just wasn't seeing it."

"It's a talent of mine." She kept her tone lighthearted. "Finding the strangest connections and confusing the heck out of whoever I'm speaking with."

"Hannah, I—"

Placing a hand on his forearm, she stilled whatever he'd been about to say. His warm skin, bronzed from the sun, had heat surging up her arm. "You've got groceries to put away." She smiled. "I have cleaning to do."

"We're having a neighborhood clambake at our place Friday night. You should stop over."

Hannah pulled her brows together. "I got the feeling from your mother that she wasn't that well acquainted with the neighbors."

He grinned. "Why do you think we're hosting a clambake?"

~

On Friday, as Hannah pulled on her boots, she promised herself that this time, if she found the house, she would walk up to the porch, say hello and get acquainted. Most of all, she would ask questions. She had so many questions.

When she left, she would make a mental note of where she was so she could find the house again.

Striding out the door, she'd reached the bottom of her steps when she heard her name being called.

Turning, she saw Charlie headed toward her.

"What are you doing up so early?" Though she wasn't one to keep track of her neighbors' comings and goings, she'd observed over the past few days that Charlie rarely made it out of his shop before five. It was barely noon.

"The clambake is today." His gaze searched hers. "You're coming."

Though he said it as a statement, she heard the question. "Wouldn't miss it."

That easy smile and warm look in his eyes were a potent duo. "Mom will be happy to hear that."

"Well," she gestured in the direction of his house when he showed no sign of returning home, "I'm sure you've got a lot to do to get ready. Is there anything I can bring?"

"Just yourself." He inclined his head. "Where are you headed?"

"I thought I'd take a walk."

A knowing look filled his brown eyes. "You're going to try to find the house."

Hannah nodded. "I thought I'd see if I can stumble across it again. Not that I've had much luck lately."

"If I weren't so busy, I'd go with you."

"Thanks, but sometimes it's more fun, and less embarrassing, for me to simply wander blindly on my own."

He chuckled as she headed toward the woods.

On impulse, Hannah looked back to find him staring after her. She offered a jaunty wave.

Pleasure spurted when he waved back.

# CHAPTER FIVE

Two hours later, Hannah returned home hot, sweaty and disappointed.

There *had* been a house in the woods. She hadn't imagined it. Or had she?

Was she losing her mind? Had she somehow resurrected the pink house of her childhood, the imaginary house filled with toys and games her father refused to buy?

*All I ever wanted was in that house.*

The house in the woods had been a different story. Women on the porch, having tea and talking? There was nothing she wanted there.

Unless, of course, she counted being able to assuage her curiosity. She should have stopped, should have taken a moment to speak to the woman who'd smiled with such warmth instead of only waving in acknowledgment.

It wasn't as if she'd had somewhere she'd needed to be at that exact moment. There had been time to stop.

Opening the refrigerator, Hannah pulled out a can of Diet Coke. Before Brian had been diagnosed, she'd given up drinking soda. That resolve hadn't lasted. The fact that she'd purchased a six-pack on her last visit to the grocery store told her she might be more stressed than she realized.

As she savored the delicious taste of her once-favorite drink, she moved to the porch swing and contemplated her options.

She could continue the search for the house. Or let it go.

Pretty simple, really.

After all, if the house *was* there, eventually she'd stumble across it again. But she wouldn't waste any more time looking for it.

There was so much to do around the house if she wanted to make it feel like *her* home. The trouble was, she was having difficulty getting motivated.

Like now, all she wanted to do was sit on the swing, sip her soda and chill.

She could almost hear Brian's voice in her head telling her to get up and do something. Make a list of what needed to get done. Set up a schedule or daily routine based on priorities. Remove distractions, then work the plan.

Brian had prided himself on being maximally productive. Hannah understood that, because being successful in sales demanded perseverance and a total focus on the goal.

For the first five years in her job, she'd pushed and pushed hard in a drive to be successful. When the boss's nephew, whom she'd trained, had gotten a promotion that should have been hers, her desire to give 110% had taken a serious hit.

Much like a football player who'd been knocked to the ground and stomped on, Hannah had found it difficult to get up. But with Brian urging her forward, she'd risen and given the job her best.

Perhaps not 110%, which she'd begun to think was ridiculous anyway, but at least 90%. Though she'd kept her eye out for other positions, the benefits and salary, plus the friends she had in the office, had kept her where she was.

Nearly a year before Brian had been diagnosed with small-cell lung cancer—if another person asked if he smoked, she was going to scream, because Brian had never smoked or lived in a home with people who smoked—Hannah had wondered if they should try to have a baby.

Though they'd agreed that their thirties would be the optimal time to start a family, what would it hurt to start trying? Especially since several of their friends had experienced difficulties getting pregnant.

Brian had been hesitant to deviate from the course they'd set. They'd still been discussing the pros and cons when their lives had imploded.

"Hey."

Hannah turned her head in the direction of the voice and pulled her thoughts back to the present.

And Charlie, who stood with a beer in one hand and a bag of Cheetos in the other. He held up the bag between two fingers and swung it back and forth. "You can't drink Coke without eating."

"I don't know that Cheetos qualify as a food source."

"I'm pretty sure they do." Charlie gestured to the swing with the hand holding the Cheetos. "Mind if I join you?"

Hannah was surprised to find she didn't mind at all. She pushed to her feet. "Sit. Let me get some paper towels. Those things are messy."

Charlie flashed a smile. "But tasty."

Hannah chuckled. "Yeah, tasty."

Inside, she washed her hands, then grabbed several paper towels, knowing one each would definitely not be enough. She'd eaten Cheetos before—actually, they were a personal favorite— and remembered the mess.

She handed some paper towels to Charlie, then took a seat. When she dipped her fingers into the open bag and took out a handful, she met his gaze. "My hands are clean."

"I was worried."

She narrowed her gaze. "Are yours?"

"Yes, ma'am." He held up both for her inspection.

"I suppose they look clean enough." She popped a Cheeto into her mouth as he scooped up a handful for himself and placed them on a paper towel in his lap. "We shouldn't be snacking this close to dinner."

"If you don't tell, I won't." He shot her a wicked smile, and she had to laugh.

After taking a sip of beer, he popped several more cheese puffs into his mouth and crunched, then drank more beer. He expelled a contented sigh. "This is how I envision heaven."

Hannah cocked her head, not sure if he was being serious or not. "Cheetos and beer? That's how you see heaven?"

"Don't forget a pretty spring day, a porch swing and good conversation."

"The only conversation we've had so far is about the Cheetos."

"That's easy enough to change." He shot her a wink. "How was your day?"

After taking another sip of her ice-cold cola, Hannah munched on several Cheetos and considered. "I'd say nonproductive."

Instead of talking to her about that being okay once in a while, but not on a regular basis, like Brian would have, Charlie simply pulled another handful of Cheetos out of the bag.

"Hey, don't eat them all."

Her protest provoked another grin. "There's plenty more."

"I did a foray into the woods." She answered his unspoken question with a sigh. "No pink house. I'm starting to wonder if I imagined it."

"Has that been a problem before?"

She frowned, not following.

"Seeing things that aren't there?" His eyes held an impish gleam. "Pink houses? Little green men?"

"I've never seen little green men."

"Not yet."

Hannah punched him in the arm and grabbed more Cheetos. She could almost see Brian shaking his head and suggesting a protein shake.

She loved protein shakes, enjoyed how she felt when she ate healthy. But she also enjoyed this. Hannah wiped her orange-tipped fingers on a paper towel.

"So, what are you saying?" She took another long sip of soda. "You don't think the pink house is real?"

"I absolutely think it's real." His tone was surprisingly matter-of-fact. "Don't you?"

She considered, but said nothing, just ate another handful.

"Just a reminder," he said, gesturing with his can of beer. "This is you and me having a conversation, not me having a conversation with myself."

She smiled. "That would be weird."

"Very weird."

"Not heavenlike at all."

"No."

"Okay, before you came over with your bag of crispy orange treats, I'd nearly convinced myself the house was only in my imagination."

"Now?"

"I think it's real." She chomped down on a Cheeto. "And tomorrow, I'm going to stay in those woods until I find it."

When Charlie and his mother did a clambake, they did it up right. Hannah gazed around the Rogan backyard in wonder.

The longest table she'd seen outside of a church soup supper sat toward the front of the backyard. The top, covered with a red-and-white-checked oilcloth and edged in lobster string lights, held a smorgasbord of food.

There were clams, mussels, crab legs and sausages. Corn on

the cob, new potatoes, onions, shallots and even artichokes. The peeled-shrimp tower sat next to a large bowl of cocktail sauce.

Several bar carts dotted the backyard. Wandering over, Hannah took note of the galvanized-steel party tub filled with ice and mini bottles of white wine as well as bottles of beer. Pitchers of iced tea, water and lemonade sat nearby.

Hannah gazed down at the lime bars she'd made that morning. They'd seemed like a good choice for a seafood-heavy menu. On what she assumed was the dessert table, she spotted a gelatin salad, fruit kebabs and what appeared to be an orange pound cake.

Though the invitation had said six o'clock, if the number of people milling around and already chowing down were any indication, she was one of the last neighbors to arrive.

A badminton net had been set up, and there was a horseshoe pit at the far back of the yard. Those areas were empty, as most of the guests appeared to be focused on eating.

Picnic tables dotted the blanket of green. People sat or stood with plates and drinks in hand. The variety of colors and styles of chairs told her many had brought their own.

"You're here." Charlie glanced down at the container in her hand. "Those look good."

"I tested one, and they taste as good as they look."

"I have no doubt." Charlie pointed. "My mom saved a seat for you next to her."

He gestured with his head toward where Lisa sat. Instead of relaxing in one of the many varieties of lawn furniture, his mother lounged in her ergonomic desk chair.

The table where Lisa sat was on the patio, instead of on the grass. Hannah assumed that was to give Charlie's mother more stable footing when she stood.

"Are you sure she wants me to—?"

"I'm sure." Charlie hesitated. "Unless you're starving, I'd like to introduce you around first."

"You don't have to introduce me," Hannah protested. "It's your party, and I'm sure you have better things to do. Besides, many of the neighbors are familiar, and the others I can meet on my own."

"Humor me." He smiled at Beverly, who strolled up. "Beverly and Geraldine helped Mom and me pull all this together."

"It was our pleasure. There's nothing we like more than a good party." Beverly, the silver in her light brown hair glistening in the late-day sun, glanced at the bars. Her eyes lit up.

"My contribution to the party," Hannah said when she noticed Beverly's interest.

"These will go quickly." Beverly lifted the container from Hannah's hands. "Thank you for bringing them."

"You're very welcome."

"How are you doing? Getting all settled?"

"I am." Hannah was conscious of Charlie standing beside her. She thought about telling him to go on and deal with his guests, but hadn't she already done that with no success? "I went for a walk in the woods today."

"Geraldine mentioned she saw you headed in that direction around noon." Beverly smiled. "The woods are lovely this time of year. We pretty much stick to the path when we walk, but when I was young, I loved to take, as they say, the road less traveled."

Hannah perked up. "You'd go off the path?"

Beverly chuckled. "Oh yes. I learned my lesson, though. I got lost—those were the days before everyone carried a phone—and I admit I was frightened. By the time I found my way out, it was dark. Geraldine was frantic and ready to call the sheriff."

"Did you ever see the house?" Hannah kept her tone offhand.

"House?" Beverly pulled her brows together. "Like a hunting cabin?"

"No, a regular house." Hannah nearly mentioned the color, but decades ago, when Beverly had been doing her exploring, it might have been a different color completely. "Two-story older home with a cupola. Two porches. One on the first story. One on the second."

"I'd have remembered seeing a house like that." Beverly slowly shook her head, her brows still furrowed in concentration. "The only structure I ever saw was the remnants of a tree house."

"Oh." Hannah offered a perfunctory smile. "I thought maybe you had."

She considered changing the subject, then realized that just because Beverly hadn't stumbled across the house didn't mean someone else hadn't mentioned to her that they had. "Did you ever hear any talk about a house in the woods?"

"No, but then, what's in the woods doesn't come up often on the committees we serve on or on the card-club circuit."

*We.* Hannah remembered all too well using *we* in conversations instead of *I*. Back then, she'd been part of a couple. Now, she flew solo.

"If you hear anyone mention anything about a house, will you let me know?" A part of Hannah wasn't sure why she persisted. After all, what she thought she'd seen that day could simply have been a figment of her imagination. Still, another part of her couldn't let it drop.

"I'll be happy to." Beverly studied her with blue eyes gone sharp and assessing. "Does someone live in this house? Or is it deserted?"

"I saw a couple of women on the porch." Hannah kept her response vague, just in case this was nothing.

A spark flared in Beverly's eyes. "Women in the woods. I can't wait to tell Geraldine."

When Hannah opened her mouth, Beverly gestured with one hand. "I'll also ask around. I'll definitely let you know if I discover anything."

"I'd appreciate it." Seeing the continued speculation in Beverly's blue eyes had Hannah adding, "I'm simply curious."

Beverly winked. "I'm the curious sort, too."

The older woman turned to Charlie. "Why don't you be a good host and introduce her around?"

Charlie's smile came easily. "I was just about to do that."

The sound of a fiddle and a banjo cut through the conversation and laughter. Hannah's gaze was drawn to a small wooden platform, barely a foot off the ground, where two musicians, one in his late forties, the other in his midteens, were tuning up.

Hannah narrowed her gaze. "Is that Dwight Richards?"

Dwight had been a programmer who'd worked for Hannah's father in the IT department at GraceTown National Lab.

"You've got a good eye. That is him, and that's his son Eli on the keyboard." Charlie grinned when the two kicked into a Beach Boys classic.

"You hired them to do background music?"

Charlie laughed, a full-throated robust sound. "Nah, Eli wants to be a full-time musician one day. He's fifteen now. He and his dad volunteer to play at different events to give him experience."

Hannah didn't recall Dwight and his wife living in the neighborhood when she'd left for college, but a lot had changed since then. "Do they live around here?"

"Down the block and around the corner." He inclined his head. "What can I get you to drink?"

"White wine?"

Striding over to the galvanized tub, he grabbed a beer for himself and one of the small bottles. Returning, he offered it to her. "Don't go all wild and crazy."

She laughed and unscrewed the cap. "No promises."

Taking a sip, she let the taste linger on her tongue and smiled.

"You like it?"

Hannah took another sip. "Not quite as satisfying as a Diet Coke and Cheetos."

"Not much compares to that." Charlie took a long pull from the beer bottle.

The laugh that rose inside Hannah felt good. "So true."

Hannah turned to see Lisa behind her, leaning on a four-pronged cane. She smiled at her hostess. "It's nice of you to have everyone over. I appreciated the invitation."

"Last year was our first in the neighborhood." Lisa glanced around the yard filled with people. "We moved in at the end of summer and had been here about a month when we decided to throw a party. This one was actually Charlie's idea."

Charlie shook his head, his eyes on his mother soft. "You did most of the planning for both."

"Did my dad and Sandie come to your party last year?" Her father had known Charlie and Brian were good friends, so it seemed odd he hadn't mentioned that Charlie and his mother lived next door.

"They, ah…" Charlie began.

"They had other plans that weekend." Lisa smiled. "Sandie and your dad had a busy social life."

"Your dad and I were well acquainted," Charlie told her. "He came over all the time when I was out in the shop."

Lisa didn't mention Sandie coming over to visit, so Hannah guessed that hadn't happened. While her stepmother was a social creature, Sandie had her friends in GraceTown. She'd once told Hannah that she wasn't particularly interested in making new ones.

According to her father, Sandie had already made a lot of new friends in Sun City. Of course, there she didn't have a choice.

"I'm betting the food stampede should slow in the next fifteen minutes." Lisa gestured to the table. "Maybe once things slow down, you can grab a plate of food and join me."

"We could eat now if you want."

"I'd like to wait until the guests get settled." Lisa paused as if a thought had just occurred to her. "Unless you're hungry and ready to eat now, then we can—"

"I had a snack midafternoon, so I'm fine," Hannah assured her. "I'll just mingle for a few minutes."

Lisa patted her arm. "You two go on ahead, then."

Startled, Hannah blurted, "I thought you'd come with us."

"You've got Charlie." Lisa gestured. "See that couple over there?"

Hannah followed the direction of Lisa's nod. "Man and woman? Early fifties?"

"They're the Sandersons, Don and Nancy. They're new to the area. They live in the house painted barn red." Lisa lifted a hand and waved at them. "I want them to feel welcome. I'll see you both soon."

As Lisa haltingly made her way across the close-cropped lawn, Hannah turned to Charlie. "You can go with her if you want. Don't feel you have to stick with me."

"It's best if she goes alone." Placing a hand lightly against the small of her back, Charlie began walking toward the back of the lawn.

"Why is that?" Curiosity had Hannah falling into step beside him.

"I don't know why it happens, but sometimes—often, really—when people see a person with a cane or a wheelchair, it makes them uncomfortable, and they end up talking to the other person."

"You think they'd talk with me or you rather than with her?"

"Odds are." Charlie shrugged. "This way, they'll get acquainted and see past the cane."

"It's hard to believe that anyone—"

"It was worse when she was in a wheelchair."

Hannah pulled her brows together. "I didn't realize your mother uses a wheelchair."

"She doesn't. Not regularly. This new medicine the doctor has her on has made a big difference. We still have the wheelchair." Charlie's tone remained matter-of-fact. "She uses it if we go anywhere where a lot of walking would be involved."

For the first time, it struck Hannah, really struck her, how lucky Lisa was to have a son like Charlie. His presence in his mother's life allowed her to maintain her independence. Or, at least as much as that was possible.

"You're a good son."

"I'm the best." He grinned. "At least that's what I tell her."

Charlie stopped just short of the horseshoe pit.

From the conversation going on between the four men standing there, their game had concluded, and they were ready for food.

"Hey, guys." Charlie's voice drew their attention. "I'd like to introduce you to Hannah Danbury. She's Leon Beahr's daughter."

Charlie introduced the men, but the names jumbled together, and a second later, Hannah couldn't recall who was who or who lived where.

"I know you're eager to eat, but I have a quick question for you." Charlie's tone remained easy. "Have any of you seen or heard of a house in the woods?"

"Like a hunting cabin?" One of the men—Hannah thought his name was Rex—asked.

"There aren't any in those woods," another said.

"Did you see a hunting cabin in the woods?" Hannah kept her voice as casual and offhand as Charlie's as she settled her gaze on Rex.

"Nope." He shrugged. "But that's the only structure I can imagine seeing there."

Hannah kept a smile on her face and nodded. She wasn't about to bring up the pink house when it was obvious none of these men had seen it. There was no point.

Rex settled his gaze on Charlie. "If you're thinking of building a house there, don't. I work at city hall, and no one is going to give you a permit to build anything in those woods. If you do build without a permit, and they find out, you'll have to tear it down."

"No worries. I've got enough to keep me busy around here."

Charlie swept out a hand in the direction of the table. "Get yourself something to eat. There is plenty there."

After a chorus of "Nice to meet you, Hannah," the men ambled across the lawn toward the food. The topic of a house in the woods had been discarded in favor of arguing over a potential foul in the last match of horseshoes.

"I could have asked the question," Hannah told Charlie.

"Tag team," was all he said before bending over to pick up two horseshoes and handing them to her. Then he reached down and grabbed two for himself.

The heavy metal felt strange in her hands. "Do you want me to put these away somewhere?"

"No." He laughed. "I want you to pitch them one at a time toward that stake. I've discovered there's nothing like a rousing game of horseshoes to work off a bag of Cheetos."

From where he stood watering the plants, Charlie saw Hannah leave her house and head in his direction.

Looking like a ray of sunshine in her blue-and-yellow-striped shirt and cropped pants, with her blond hair pulled back in a tail, she lifted her lips in a bright smile when she spotted him.

He felt the punch.

The intensity of his reaction took him by surprise. He'd had limited contact with her when she'd first become engaged to Brian and then married him. Back then, he hadn't given her more than a passing thought.

She'd been friendly, but reserved. A couple of times, he'd caught her looking from him to Brian as if trying to figure out how they were friends.

She seemed different now. Maybe it was maturity. She and Brian had been so young when they married. Or maybe he had changed. Charlie decided the why didn't really matter.

The fact that they could enjoy each other's company made being neighbors a thousand times easier.

"You look ready to face the day." He turned off the nozzle on the hose before shifting toward her.

"I've already faced it." The easy smile remained on her face, and he noticed the strain that had bracketed her eyes when she'd first moved in was gone. "I grabbed a latte with Mackenna, then we got our toes done."

She extended her sandaled foot, and he saw a flash of bright red.

"Looks good."

"I'm happy with how they turned out." She gestured to the rosebush he'd been watering. "I remember the owner of the Burger Shack, where I worked in high school, gave me a potted rosebush for my birthday. My dad told me they took too much time and effort and wouldn't let me plant it."

"What did you do?"

"I kept it going in my room for the longest time." She lifted a shoulder, let it drop. "I don't remember exactly what led to its demise."

"Roses take work. They're prone to powdery mildew, rust and black spot. But those issues are easily managed if you're diligent. Besides, my mom loves them." Enough about his mother, Charlie thought. Sometimes it felt like she was the only thing he and Hannah ever discussed. "What else is on your agenda for today?"

She inclined her head. "Does one always need a plan?"

"Not really. At least not a detailed one." Charlie set down the hose and wiped his hands on his jeans. "I usually have some idea what I want to do during the day. Like today." He gestured to the plants. "I like to water early so the sun has time to dry off any excess moisture before the evening."

Great, he thought. Now they were discussing roses.

"I didn't realize that. Since my father wasn't into flowering plants—"

"Too much work." Charlie flashed a smile. "I get it."

"They are lovely, though." She reached down to finger a soft pink petal. "Well, despite what I just said about not always needing a plan, I have one, of sorts. I'm making a list of everything I want to change in the house. You know, to make it feel like mine."

Charlie nodded. He'd had a feeling that she would want to make changes. While Hannah's father had kept the home clean and maintained, he hadn't been one for doing much more than that. "What's first?"

"I thought I'd start with the floors and walls." She laid out her plan for the main level.

He listened and offered a nod every now and then, most often accompanied by an encouraging murmur. He liked the way her eyes sparkled as she spoke of paint samples and window treatments.

"Which leads me to why I came over." She expelled a breath. "I've been gone so long I don't know who I should contact about refinishing floors or painting. I thought perhaps your mother might have a few suggestions. I would have called, but I don't have her number."

"You could have just called me."

"I, ah, I tossed out that box without writing down your number."

"I can give you both of ours again. That way, you have them, not only for stuff like this, but for emergencies."

This time, she entered both numbers into her phone. He didn't ask for hers, so she just gave it to him.

"Don't feel you need to call or text before you pop by every time," he told her. "Just come over. My mom and I both like company."

"I know you both work, and I wouldn't want to—"

"I'd say 99% of what we do can be set aside at any given time."

"Okay." Her hands fluttered in the air as if she wasn't sure what to do with them. "Good to know."

"You'll want to do the floors first. Paint isn't difficult to clean off a well-finished floor, but dust from sanding can collect on newly painted walls." Charlie considered who he'd recommend. "Do you remember Harley Sparks?"

"Vaguely." She shrugged. "I don't think I'd recall him at all if not for the weird name."

"He was two years ahead of us in school." Charlie smiled, thinking of all the nicknames the guy had had to endure during his childhood. "He went into the floor-refinishing business with his dad. Sparks & Son Floors, with Harley being the son. They are one of the biggest contractors of their kind in GraceTown."

"But my house—"

"Though their focus is more on the commercial side, they do a fair amount of residential," Charlie interrupted. "From every-thing I've heard, they do amazing work, and their prices are competitive."

"I suppose I could contact them." Hannah chewed on her

bottom lip. "Though I bet they're booked up."

"Remind Harley that Brian was your husband. Harley played ball with me and Brian. He'll take on the job." There wasn't a single doubt in Charlie's mind of that fact.

Hannah grew quiet.

"Problem?"

"I wouldn't feel comfortable bringing up Brian."

While that didn't make sense to Charlie, he had a work-around. "How 'bout I call him up, let him know my neighbor is looking for someone and see if he's got a crew available? If he does, I'll give you your number, and you can work out the details with him."

"You wouldn't mind?"

"Not at all. Quick five-minute call, and you'll be on your way, and if not, I can give you the names of other contractors you can trust to treat you right."

"Thanks so much, Charlie." Hannah placed a hand on his bicep and gave a squeeze. "I really appreciate this."

"When you're ready for the walls, I can give you some names there."

Hannah nodded, opened her mouth to speak, but shut it again.

"Something wrong?" Charlie asked.

"No, it's just that if someone had told me in high school that one day you and I would be trading tips on gardening and home repair, I never would have believed them."

"Well, technically, I'm the only one actually offering advice, so I don't think you can call this 'trading.'"

Hannah laughed. "You know what I mean. Coming back to GraceTown, finding you next door, it's very…"

"Very what?"

"Unexpected. All of it. You."

Charlie grinned. "You're not what I expected either. Isn't it great?"

# CHAPTER SEVEN

Back at home, Hannah spent the next couple of hours online, losing herself in paint possibilities.

When her stomach grumbled, she tossed together some lunch, then opened the windows, letting the warm breeze and fresh scents that were June in Maryland wash over her.

Being inside on such a beautiful day made no sense. Not when this was the perfect afternoon for exploring. She'd just decided to pull out her hiking boots when she got a text from Emma.

*Got time to talk?*

Something must be up for Emma to want an actual conversation. Her friend usually preferred texting over talking.

Apparently not today, though.

*Yes.* Hannah included a smiley-face emoji in her response.

The phone rang a second later.

"Emma. Hello. It's good to hear from you."

"Ditto. How are things back in the old hometown?"

Emma's voice held an excited edge. Hannah knew her friend too well to think this would be just a random call. Emma had news to share.

"Things are going well." Hannah glanced out the window and spotted Charlie standing beside a motorcycle, chatting with a scruffy-looking man with a long gray beard.

She wasn't sure what Charlie did for a living, but shouldn't he be working?

*Not my business.* Hannah returned her attention to the conversation at hand. "I've got big changes planned for my home's interior. Beginning with having the wood floors refinished. I'm also looking at paint options."

She was about to add that she was considering planting rosebushes and realized she was on the verge of rambling. Hannah clamped her lips together.

"Don't tell me you're actually going to paint over the white?" Emma pretended to gasp. "What is your dad going to think?"

Hannah had told her friend all about her father's proclivities.

"Dear old Dad won't know until he returns for a visit, and by then, it will be a fait accompli." Hannah smiled. "I'm sure he'll love it, and I'm really looking forward to having some color in here. Enough about me. How are things in Greensboro?"

"Same. Except..." The excited quiver was back in Emma's voice. "I've got fabulous news. Calista and Jack are pregnant. We're doing a girls' lunch next weekend to celebrate. I wish you were here so you could come with us."

Calista was an inner-circle friend. Hannah had first met the stylish brunette when Emma had invited Hannah to join a monthly Wine, Women and Wit book club, in which the two were both members. She'd liked Calista instantly. The woman had an upbeat outlook on life and a dry sense of humor.

When Calista had left her retail management position to pursue a long-held dream of becoming an attorney, Hannah had cheered her on.

"I'm thrilled for both her and Jack. I wish I could be there to give her a big hug and tell her congrats in person." Hannah already knew what kind of celebratory cupcakes she'd bake to give to the happy couple if she'd still been in Greensboro. "Where's the luncheon?"

"Green Valley Grill."

"Yum." The restaurant, with its wood-fired rotisserie and grill, was a favorite. "I love their blackberry mojitos."

"Their scallops aren't half bad either."

"I miss the scallops." Hannah couldn't count the number of times when Brian had been working late that she and Emma had stopped into the Grill and split an entrée of the pan-seared scallops for dinner. Hannah smiled at the sweet memory before pulling her brows together. "I'm happy, but a bit surprised to hear they're pregnant. I thought Calista said they'd decided to wait until she was out of law school to start a family."

"Best-laid plans." Emma chuckled. "Calista told me this baby was obviously meant to be. They're both so excited. Jack has already compiled a list of baby names."

"It's going to be rough with her still in school—"

"You're right. Now isn't the best time, but they're rolling with it."

*Now isn't the best time.*

Nearly the same words that Brian had uttered two years ago when Hannah had mentioned wanting to start a family. Or, at least, wanting to go off birth control and try.

Hannah fought a pang of envy. "I'll text Calista, but please give her my congrats and best wishes."

When the conversation ended, Hannah sat, staring at the phone in her hand.

Two years ago, Hannah had hoped that by now she'd be the one with the pregnancy news. Instead, she was back in her hometown without her husband or a child.

With each passing year, she was learning just how unpredictable and capricious life could be. Unexpected occurrences could derail carefully made plans, not to mention hopes and dreams.

Hannah thought of Charlie's stance that the unexpected was "great." She wondered how, with everything that had happened to his mother, even with what had happened to his best friend, he could keep that outlook.

Shoving all thoughts of what might have been aside, Hannah hurried upstairs to grab her hiking boots. She needed to stop thinking and start moving.

And maybe, just maybe, today she would get lucky and find the pink house again.

～

Instead of letting her mind wander as she strode through the woods, Hannah paid close attention to where she was. She took note of a log covered in a filmy moss, a tree where someone had carved their initials and, most of all, the various directions she headed.

Anticipating that it might take some time before she found the house, she set aside the entire afternoon to search. She found the home in under thirty minutes.

The sun streaming through the thick trees cast a golden glow over the beautiful house, making the pink brighter, the blooms of the flowering plants more vibrant.

After taking pictures, Hannah pocketed her phone and stepped into the clearing.

Only one woman sat on the porch today. Hannah was relieved to see that she was the friendly blonde, her hair pulled back in a braid that hung down her back.

Catching sight of Hannah, the woman lifted her hand in greeting.

Returning the wave, Hannah strode to the house on surprisingly shaky legs. "Good afternoon."

"It's a gorgeous day, isn't it?" The woman's friendly smile put

Hannah instantly at ease. "You look warm. Would you like to sit for a spell? I've got sun tea."

For the first time, Hannah noticed the pitcher and two glasses sitting on the table.

"I'd like that," Hannah said quickly. "As long as I'm not intruding..."

"Not at all." The woman poured a glass for Hannah, then one for herself. She gestured to the empty chair. "Please, have a seat."

"Thank you." Hannah settled herself in the wicker chair and offered a smile. "I'm Hannah—"

"Maisie." The woman extended her hand.

When Hannah wrapped her fingers around the slender hand, a feeling of warmth stole over her. In that moment, she knew that continuing to search for the house had been the right move.

"I tried several times to find my way back here." Hannah gave a little laugh. "I discovered that even a pink house can be difficult to find."

As if she'd heard that comment before, Maisie smiled and lifted the glass of tea to her red lips.

"Where are your friends?" Hannah asked.

The woman arched a brow.

"The women you were with the last time I came by."

Maisie waved a hand. "They come and go."

"So this is your house?"

"For now." Maisie inclined her head. "Tell me about Hannah."

The intense curiosity in the woman's gaze surprised her.

Hannah set down the glass. "There isn't much to tell."

"Oh, I'm sure that's not true."

"I guess you can be the judge." Hannah relaxed against the seatback. The porch had a roof over it, the ceiling as blue as the sky. Why did that fact comfort and soothe? She smiled at Maisie and prepared to give the woman a condensed version of her life over the past decade.

"I grew up not far from here in GraceTown," Hannah began. "You're familiar with the community?"

It seemed a silly question. Living so close, how could she not be? Still, Hannah didn't want to assume.

"I am." Maisie's friendly smile showed a mouthful of straight white teeth. Laugh lines, whisper-fine, edged her eyes.

"Well, I left for college right after high school. I obtained a degree in business from UNC at Chapel Hill. I met my husband, Brian, there. He also happened to be from GraceTown. We fell in love and married right after college graduation."

Back then, Hannah's life had been bright and filled with endless possibilities. Never, ever had she imagined her time with Brian would be cut short. A familiar tightness wrapped around Hannah's chest, making breathing difficult.

In and out. In and out. She forced herself to breathe, to steady.

"He's no longer with you."

Startled, Hannah forgot all about getting air into her lungs. "What?"

"Your husband. He's no longer with you."

Hannah stilled. "How do you know that?"

Maisie only cocked her head.

Hannah decided Maisie's assumption must have something to do with her voice. Both Emma and Mackenna had mentioned on more than one occasion that something changed when she spoke Brian's name.

"Brian was diagnosed with cancer last year. He passed away six weeks later." As Hannah inhaled the sweet scent of lily of the valley, the tightness in her chest lessened, and she found she could once again breathe easily.

"I'm very sorry for your loss." The woman's blue eyes, the same blue green as her own, met Hannah's. "I realize they're just words, but I know how it feels to lose someone you love."

Before Hannah could ask who Maisie had lost, the woman continued. "This past year was a difficult one for you."

"It was." Mouth now bone-dry, Hannah gulped down tea. "I stayed in North Carolina after Brian's death. We lived in Greensboro our entire married life. I could have moved back to Grace-Town, but my job and my friends were there and—"

Hannah hesitated, remembering how going back to work at Mingus after the funeral had not only steadied her, but it had also given purpose to her fractured life.

"You didn't want any more changes." Maisie's softly spoken words reached deep, rooting out Hannah's greatest fear.

"Honestly, I didn't believe I could handle one more change." Hannah glanced down at her hands, now twisted in her lap. "Then I got RIF'd."

"RIF'd?" Maisie's brows pulled together.

"Reduced in Force. It's like being fired, but not. The employee hasn't done anything wrong. The company just needs—or wants —to reduce personnel."

"Despite knowing it wasn't personal, I bet losing a position you'd held for so many years felt very personal."

Had she told Maisie how long she'd been at Mingus? Or had the woman simply assumed? Did it really matter?

Something about Maisie's calm manner put Hannah at ease and encouraged her to share confidences.

"After Brian's death, losing my position at Mingus—that's the name of the company I worked for—felt very much like another loss. Not of the same magnitude as losing the man I loved, but still a loss."

Hannah blew out a breath and fought for composure. The woman had asked a simple question. Why did she feel the need to bare her soul?

Maisie nodded, sympathy shimmering in her kind eyes.

Tears threatened, but Hannah blinked rapidly so they wouldn't fall. "Coming so close to the anniversary of my husband's death, well, that was a difficult time."

"I can imagine." Maisie's voice was as gentle as a mother's caress.

"I didn't believe I could go on, but 'in the midst of winter, I found there was, within me—'"

"'An invincible summer.'"

"You know the Albert Camus quote." The author's quote was a favorite of Hannah's and one she clung to as she tentatively negotiated a life suddenly gone dark.

Maisie met her gaze. "It says so much."

Hannah nodded. "Brian was gone. My job was history. The townhouse where we lived was nice, but it had never really felt like home. At least not a permanent home. Other than friends, there was nothing keeping me in North Carolina. Then my father decided to move to Florida and offered me the family home. It was incredibly generous, but—"

Understanding filled Maisie's eyes when Hannah's voice trailed off. "Returning to GraceTown would be another change."

"Yes." Hannah paused. "When I hesitated, my father had difficulty understanding why I wasn't jumping at the offer."

Several beats of silence ensued that Maisie made no attempt to fill.

"It *was* generous," Hannah added. "It was just…"

Hannah fluttered a hand in the air.

This time, Maisie filled in the blank. "Another change."

"Yes." Hannah sighed.

"Did you explain your feelings to your father?" Maisie probed, her voice as soft as silk.

"I tried. My dad is a computer guy, very analytical. He's a wonderful man, but emotions aren't his forte." Hannah realized the woman hadn't yet asked about her mother. To circumvent that, she added, "My mom died when I was young."

"She loved you very much."

"That's what everyone who knew her tells me."

"The fact that you're sitting here now tells me you decided to return to GraceTown."

Hannah gazed out over the forest of trees. "I must be getting good at change, because the move wasn't as difficult as I anticipated."

"Coming home was the right decision."

"It was," Hannah agreed. Inside the large home, a clock chimed the hour, the sound reminding Hannah that she was an unexpected guest. The last thing she wanted to do was overstay her welcome. "I should be going."

When she started to rise, Maisie placed a staying hand on her arm. "Before you do, I have something to give you." Maisie rose with an easy elegance. "I'll be right back."

While she waited, Hannah listened to the sounds of the forest —the chatter of squirrels, a birdsong she couldn't quite identify and the pleasant sound of wind rustling through the trees.

Hannah found herself wishing she could linger. There was something soothing about the beautiful pink house and its owner.

Maisie returned with an envelope. When she held out her hand, Hannah saw her own name scrawled across the front, the looping style distinctive—and familiar.

For a second, Hannah's heart simply stopped. Then it started again, but hard and fast, too fast.

Maisie placed a supportive hand on Hannah's shoulder. "It's okay. Just breathe. Slow and steady."

"That's…" Hannah looked up at the woman through widened eyes. "Brian's handwriting."

Maisie nodded.

"Where did you get this?" Hannah demanded, her voice pitching high.

"Does it matter where it came from?" Maisie met Hannah's questioning gaze with a steady one of her own. "What matters is you have it now."

# CHAPTER EIGHT

Hannah longed to see what was inside the envelope. But she wanted to do so in private, not under Maisie's watchful gaze.

Her world, which had steadied over the past weeks, had once again been knocked off its axis. "I'm going home."

Maisie nodded. "I understand."

Hannah held up the envelope, now clutched tightly in her hand. "Thank you for this."

"You're welcome." Maisie's expression remained focused on her until Hannah disappeared into the woods.

Her mind continued to race as she tried to make sense of something that made no sense. How had an envelope addressed to her ended up at a house in the middle of the woods? Did mail even get delivered here?

Even if it did, there was no address on the envelope, just her name.

With each step she took toward home, Hannah's heartrate increased. By the time she burst out of the woods, her breath came in short puffs, as if she'd just run a long race.

Someone called her name.

She paid no attention. Right now, nothing mattered except

getting inside her house—her sanctuary—and opening the envelope.

After unlocking the door—it took two attempts due to her hands refusing to stop shaking—she made it inside. She dropped down on the sofa, the envelope still clutched in one hand.

When she'd taken it from Maisie, she thought the flap had been sealed. It was, but so lightly she was able to run her finger under the edge and open it without any real effort.

A folded piece of parchment lay inside.

Taking a steadying breath, Hannah grasped the paper with two fingers, slipping out the single sheet and unfolding it.

*My dearest Hannah.*

She had to pause, had to force herself to breathe even as tears filled her eyes, and her heart became a sweet mass in her chest.

Brian, her beloved husband, had written this letter. To her.

When had he done this? Had it been before or after that horrible day when she'd rushed him to the hospital because he was coughing up blood and fighting for breath? That was when they'd learned Brian wasn't battling bronchitis or pneumonia, but something far worse.

Hannah had been with him every day of his fight to survive and had been holding his hand when he passed.

Inhaling a shuddering breath, she cast aside the questions and read.

*My dearest Hannah,*

*As we've both discovered, the future is not guaranteed. I thought I had all the time in the world with you. It wasn't to be.*

*Do you remember when I proposed? On that sunny day, life stretched before us like a huge blank canvas filled with possibilities. We were so practical. Too practical, I realize now.*

*Remember our plan? It seemed to make so much sense. Focus on careers in our twenties. Focus on building a family in our thirties. Again, that big blank canvas offered infinite possibilities.*

*Instead of being so practical, we could have been traveling the world.*

*We could have been making babies. We could have been enjoying our youth.*

*The plans we made together were cut short. I think of all the time we gave our jobs and wonder now what any of it was for.*

*You were coming into your own when we started dating in college. I wanted to give you a full life, a happy life.*

*If only we'd had more time together. I wish I'd approached you back when we were kids so there was never a part of my life that you weren't with me.*

*There are so many things that were a part of my life back then that I would have shared with you.*

*Fishing on Pigeon Creek at dawn.*

*Eating a snowball at the Frederick County Fair.*

*Swimming at Devil's Bathtub.*

*If I'd had more time, I'd have taken you to all those places and more, because these are where I was the happiest. All I ever wanted was to bring you that same happiness.*

*I want that for you now.*

*I want you to be happy.*

There was no signature. It wasn't necessary. Hannah knew Brian had written the words. To her.

Tears slipped down her cheeks. She hoped Brian didn't think that she regretted any of the time they'd shared. They'd been happy together. They'd had a wonderful life together. How could they have known their time together would be cut so short?

A brisk knock at the door had Hannah's head jerking up. She swiped at her damp cheeks with the pads of her fingers.

Folding the letter, she placed it with the envelope on the coffee table before standing and calling out, "Who is it?"

"Charlie. May I come in?"

Hannah didn't want to see him now. Didn't want to see anyone. She wanted to sit in the darkened room and cry over unfulfilled dreams. Only now did she realize she hadn't turned on any lights. No matter, there had been enough light from the outside for her to read the letter.

"Is everything okay?"

The concern in Charlie's voice had Hannah opening the door.

"Hi, Charlie." She could have cheered when her voice came out steady. "What can I do for you?"

His gaze, sharp and assessing, took in her tear-stained face and trembling hands.

Try as she might, Hannah hadn't been able to still the shaking that came from deep within.

"Did you find the house?"

She blinked.

"Did you find the pink house?" He jerked his head in the direction of the woods.

"I did." The visit had been lovely, until Maisie had given her the envelope.

"I thought as much." Charlie narrowed his gaze. "Did the people hurt you?"

"People?"

"The ones at the house."

"It was just one woman today, and no," she shook her head, "she didn't hurt me. We had a nice conversation on the porch."

"Good. That's good." The tense set to his jaw eased slightly as he rocked back on his heels. "Then what's the matter?"

"Who says anything is the matter?"

The look he shot her told her to give it to him straight.

"Right before I left, Maisie—that's the woman's name—gave me a letter."

Charlie arched a dark brow. "Who from?"

"From Brian."

～

Charlie's brows slammed together like two storm clouds ready to rumble. "What kind of sick joke is she playing?"

Without any thought, Hannah stepped aside.

As if taking the action as an invitation for him to enter, Charlie brushed past her, flicking the light switch on as he passed. The glow from the lamps chased away lingering shadows, but the chill inside her remained.

Hannah shivered. Despite the words of love she'd read, the sorrow, that deep, dark wave that had once threatened to pull her under, tugged at her now. With her arms wrapped tightly around herself, she felt like she was losing the battle.

"Hannah."

She looked up and stared into warm brown eyes.

The look in those eyes was as steady as the hand he rested on her shoulder. "What can I do?"

"Can you hold me? For just a minute?"

Without a word, his arms encircled her, and she tilted her head against his broad chest. She stayed that way for several heartbeats, absorbing his strength and letting the warmth of his body drive away the chill.

Once she steadied, Hannah stepped back.

Even as his arms fell to his sides, his gaze never left her face. "Can I get you something to drink? Water? Coffee? A shot of whiskey?"

She had to chuckle.

At the sound, the concern in his eyes lessened.

"I'm not much of a drinker, but I sure could use a shot of Jack right about now."

"I've got a bottle at my house," Charlie assured her. "It will just take a second for me to—"

Hannah wasn't sure what got into her. She grasped his hand as one might a lifeline. "Don't go."

"Not going anywhere." He'd kept his tone light, but worry returned to his brown eyes. "May I see the letter?"

Swallowing hard, she gestured with one hand to the coffee table.

He placed a hand on her arm, the touch as gentle as his voice. "Let's give it a look."

When she sat on the sofa, Charlie dropped down beside her. Picking up the letter, she handed it to him.

"Seeing Brian's handwriting, reading his words..." Hannah blinked rapidly. "I thought I'd grieved enough for one lifetime. But then I get hit with something like this, and the pain rushes back. You probably don't understand..."

"I never lost a spouse, but my grandpa, my mom's dad, he and I were close." Charlie's eyes turned dark with memories. "Even now, twenty years later, I'll be working on something and swear I feel Pops looking over my shoulder, ready to offer a suggestion." Charlie's smile held both sadness and love. "Though not as strong as when he first passed, that's when the grief will hit me."

"He sounds like a wonderful man."

"He was. My mom told me once that grief is the price of love."

Hannah nodded. She took in a breath and let it out slowly. "Maisie was kind to me."

"You said the two of you had a conversation on the porch. Then what? She pulls out this letter?"

Charlie held the sheet of paper loosely between his fingers, but made no move to read it. It was as if he realized she needed more time to settle.

Hannah scrubbed her face with her hands, trying to clear her brain of the muddle. "We actually talked for quite a while, mostly about the changes in my life—Brian's illness and death, losing my job and moving."

"Then she comes up with this letter and says it's from your husband?"

"She handed me the envelope. I saw my name." Hannah's lips wanted to tremble, but she pressed them together until they steadied. "Look at it, Charlie. It's Brian's handwriting."

His gaze dropped to the envelope, and she heard his quick inhale.

"You see it, too." Her heart fluttered. "Brian had a distinctive way of making his H's."

"He did. That's his handwriting." Charlie lifted his head and met her gaze. "How can this be?"

For someone who normally had all the answers, Charlie appeared equally thunderstruck.

"I asked Maisie where she got it. She said something like, 'Does it matter? You've got it now.'" Hannah raked a hand through her hair. "I probably should have pressed, but once I saw it was Brian's handwriting, I found it hard to think."

"What happened then?" he prompted.

"I came home. I opened the envelope and read the letter."

"I'm sorry you had to face this alone." His voice held a gravelly quality she hadn't heard before.

She lifted her chin. "I can handle it."

"I have no doubt of that." His matter-of-fact tone was just what she needed. "But being there during tough times is what friends are for."

Was Charlie a friend? Yes, she concluded, he was. And, of all her friends, she was glad he was the one with her now.

Charlie continued to hold the paper loosely in his large hand. "Is it okay with you if I read this?"

There were words of love in the letter as well as regret. But Charlie had been Brian's best friend since childhood. If anyone could give her insight, it would be him.

"'My dearest Hannah,'" he read, then looked up. "This letter is clearly meant for you. No doubt there."

She nodded, hoping he wasn't planning on reading the entire letter aloud. Hearing Brian's words on his lips would seem wrong somehow. If he began to read aloud, she'd stop him.

It wasn't necessary.

# CHAPTER NINE

Charlie was impressed. Hannah had taken pictures and made careful notes on her phone of the route she'd taken to find the pink house. The pictures of the house? Well, those were a blur.

The path was a familiar one. He and Brian had done their share of exploring these woods over the years. Charlie swore if there was a pink house anywhere close, he'd have seen it.

After thirty minutes, Hannah stopped and turned to him. Obviously bewildered, she turned in a circle, then pointed. "This is where the house should be. But it's not."

"Are you sure we didn't take a wrong turn somewhere?"

"I'm positive." Her hands clenched in frustration. "I don't understand how it could have been here earlier, and now it's not."

Her voice pitched high.

Perhaps coming here so soon after reading the letter had been a mistake. Charlie had to admit that seeing Brian's handwriting and reading the words his friend had written had been like a sledge to the chest.

All that Brian had wished he'd had a chance to show Hannah were things he and Charlie had shared growing up.

Such amazing memories.

He understood why Brian had longed to share those adventures with his wife.

Sitting in Hannah's living room, he'd nearly mentioned that those adventures had been part of his childhood, too, and that he'd be happy to share them with her.

Charlie had kept his mouth shut. It would have seemed wrong for him to insert himself in those experiences. Except, he doubted Hannah would ever experience swimming at Devil's Bathtub if he didn't intervene, not with her aversion to violating Mr. Jessup's sign.

Charlie knew Merle Jessup. He'd helped him out only last month when the man's ancient snowblower had needed repairing. He had no doubt if he asked Merle if he could bring a friend to the swimming hole, the old man would make an exception to his keep-off-my-property rule.

Hannah turned to him, tears shimmering in her blue eyes. "What if I can never find the pink house again?"

"You found it twice," he reminded her. "You'll find it again. Just not today."

Hannah found planting a rosebush at the corner of her house the next day steadied her. Since getting the letter yesterday, Brian's words were all she could think about.

She'd called Emma last night to check in and see how things were going. They talked for nearly an hour, mostly about Calista and some drama at Emma's job.

Hannah hadn't brought up the letter.

Emma would be even more of a skeptic than Mackenna. Emma was in Greensboro. She didn't know Brian's handwriting and couldn't see the letter for herself or hold it in her hands.

A pink house. A letter from her deceased husband.

It sounded farfetched even to Hannah. She was glad that

Charlie had been the one to stop over when she'd gotten home. Glad that she'd let him read the letter.

Like her, Charlie had recognized Brian's handwriting. And the activities that Brian had mentioned in the letter were familiar to him.

The fact that she hadn't been able to find the pink house again, despite her notes, hadn't shaken his faith that the house was real and the letter was from Brian.

Her phone buzzed just as she finished packing the rich, dark soil around the bush. Taking off her gardening gloves, Hannah pulled out her phone.

It was a text from Mackenna.

*Want to go to the GraceTown Fair?*

For a second, Hannah was confused why her friend had the day free. Then she realized today was Sunday.

*Say where and when.*

As the fairgrounds were equidistant from each of their homes, it made sense to meet there.

*Red barn near the entrance in 30?*

Hannah considered. *Make it 45.*

The thumbs-up emoji came seconds later.

Taking a shower and slapping on makeup would take twenty. Then there was the drive. If she'd had to, Hannah could have done a quick shower, but she didn't want to rush. As she didn't need to hurry, she lingered, letting warm water stream over her skin and relax her tight muscles.

As she stood there, face lifted to the spray, Hannah let her mind wander back to the letter. She vowed to take to heart Brian's warning that the future was not guaranteed.

~

The fairgrounds were crowded, noisy and just what Hannah needed. She found Mackenna easily, the redhead striking in white shorts and a bright yellow shirt.

Hannah waved. She couldn't recall if Mackenna liked rides, but just in case, she'd worn shorts instead of a dress.

Mackenna gave her a hug. "I'm so glad you could meet me."

Hugging her back, Hannah gave thanks for Brian's letter. The kick in the backside that it had given her to seize the moment was what had prompted her to accept Mackenna's invitation today.

"I'm excited." Hannah looked around. "Where to first?"

Mackenna offered a sheepish grin. "I heard the fish display is back this year. You know, the tanks filled with fish from Maryland waters? It shouldn't take long, but for some crazy reason, I love looking at them."

"Those tanks are a must-see for me, too," Hannah admitted. "I love the catfish."

"The rainbow trout are my fav."

Hannah thought of the letter. "Do you fish?"

"Me?" Mackenna brought a hand to her chest and fluttered her lash extensions. "Do I look like someone who'd bait a hook with a worm or something equally gross?"

Hannah took that as a no. Which meant Mackenna wouldn't be any help in the fishing arena. She could do some reading. See if Charlie maybe had a pole or a rod she could borrow...

"What about you?"

Hannah shook her head. "Sitting in a boat or on a bank always seemed kind of boring to me. Even if I caught one, I'd just throw it back."

Ignoring a prominently displayed warning sign, Mackenna tapped the glass side of a tank. "This is as close as I want to get."

"Amen."

The sentiment had Mackenna chuckling and slanting Hannah

a sideways glance. "What have you been doing to keep yourself busy this week?"

Keeping busy had been her and Brian's focus for nearly a decade. Maximizing time. Being productive. Taking advantage of every spare minute to get some work done.

"Nothing exciting," Hannah answered. "A little baking, some cleaning and a whole lot of planning. I've also planted a few flowers and gone for a couple walks in the woods. What about you?"

"Work has been crazy. The days fly by. That's the way I like it." Mackenna paused in front of the catfish display and pointed with a long red nail to a particularly large flathead. "He reminds me of Mr. Petree."

Hannah remembered their social studies teacher with his broad, jowly face and a mustache he'd greased and curled. She chuckled. "Very much so."

"Hey, Petree." Mackenna tapped on the glass, then shrugged when the fish swam off. "Brian was in that class with us. Remember? He and Charlie sat in the back."

Now that her friend had brought it up, Hannah did remember. Of course, back in high school, she, even more so than Mackenna, had been firmly entrenched in what Hannah thought of as the middle tier of popularity.

Charlie and Brian had been at the top. The athletes. The good-looking guys who'd known how to have a good time. Boys who'd always had a pithy response.

When they'd gotten acquainted in college, Brian had told Hannah she'd always been on his radar. It was nice of him to say, but she wasn't sure she believed him.

"Neither of them knew I existed."

Mackenna laughed. "Yeah, right."

"Neither of them did," Hannah insisted, wondering why she'd brought Charlie into the conversation.

"You were the one who didn't know they existed," Mackenna

said pointedly. "You were more into your studies than socializing."

"That's because no one asked me to do anything." Hannah chuckled, not bitter, but not wanting to sugarcoat either.

"You had that air of 'don't ask' back then." Mackenna's gaze grew thoughtful. "I'd have taken you with me to some of the parties, but you gave no indication of wanting to go. It was as if—and don't take this the wrong way—such things were beneath you."

The words brought a tiny pinprick of pain to Hannah's heart. If she'd been more open to possibilities, could she and Brian have been together back then?

"I'm sorry, Hannah." Mackenna grabbed her arm. "I didn't mean to hurt your—"

"No, no," Hannah hastened to reassure her. "You didn't. Well, maybe a little, but only because I remember when Brian and I first started dating in college, he said something similar. I just fluffed it off because I thought, 'No, I'm not like that.' But maybe I was…"

"You knew who you were and what you wanted, even back then. A lot of kids lose their way in high school. You never did."

"Maybe." Hannah saw no reason to admit that she also hadn't had much fun during those years. Still, college had been wonderful, as had her life with Brian, until his illness had blindsided them.

Gesturing to the double Ferris wheel in the distance, Hannah changed the subject. "The first time I went up in one of those, it was with you. Remember?"

Done with the fish, she and Mackenna made their way toward the large wheel. They skirted vendors selling toys that drew the eye but would likely fall apart in a week and those hawking various petitions needing signatures.

Every ten feet or so, they were stopped by someone who knew Mackenna. There would be introductions and polite conversation. Hannah hoped by next year as many people would stop to speak with her.

"It appears all paths lead to the Midway." Hannah gestured with one hand toward the monster rides zipping and zooming through the air up ahead.

"Do you mind if we stop and get something to drink first?" Mackenna turned toward a village of white wooden food huts ahead. "I'm craving a frozen lemonade."

Hannah smiled. "I could go for something cold."

They stopped at a hut with a huge cup of frozen lemonade painted on the side. A large board listing all the available products told Hannah that this stand sold a whole lot more than lemonade.

"Mackenna. Hannah." Charlie stood behind the counter, a day's worth of dark scruff on his cheeks. "What can I get you?"

"Hey, Charlie." Mackenna flashed a bright smile. "How've you been?"

"Good." He slanted a glance at Hannah, then returned his attention to Mackenna. "I don't know what you ladies are in the mood for, but our piña colada snowballs are extremely popular."

Mackenna wrinkled her nose. "Frozen lemonade for me."

Hannah's thoughts went back to the letter.

*Eating a snowball at the Frederick County Fair.*

Though this wasn't the Frederick County Fair, and Brian wasn't with her, she'd have a snowball in his memory.

"Snowball for me," Hannah told Charlie.

"What flavor?" Charlie pointed to the list on the board.

"Though I'm tempted to go with cherry—"

"Boring," Charlie interjected.

"—give me the piña colada," Hannah finished.

"Good choice. If you don't like it, I'll make you another," he promised.

"Hey," Mackenna protested. "Last year when I wished I'd gotten lime instead of cherry, you didn't give me another one."

Hannah cocked her head. "Last year?"

"Charlie works the Rotary stand every year." Mackenna appeared puzzled. "Back in high school, we'd always stop by to see him."

Hannah shook her head and shrugged.

"I guess I'm forgettable." Charlie chuckled as he handed over their orders. "Where are you two headed?"

Mackenna glanced up at the screams coming from a plummeting roller coaster, then lifted a shoulder. "The rides, I guess."

"We don't have to if you don't want to." Hannah spoke quickly. "I can take 'em or leave 'em. We can—"

She stopped when she realized her friend was no longer listening. Mackenna's gaze was firmly focused on a dark-haired man holding the hand of a little girl. "I see someone I know. Wait for me. I'll be right back."

Hannah wasn't sure what to think when her friend hurried off at a fast clip, slowing her steps only when she drew close to the duo.

"You're wondering why she didn't ask you to go with her."

Hannah blinked, then refocused on Charlie. While she didn't want to keep him from his work, she noticed no customers were waiting. "Maybe."

"Mackenna has a thing for Jace Tanner. He's the only one who doesn't know it."

"Does she?" Hannah dipped the spoon into the top of the snowball and took a bite. The shaved ice, saturated with piña colada flavor, melted in her mouth. "Hey, this is good."

That easy smile flashed again. "Brian would definitely approve of your choice."

"Probably." She wondered if Charlie was thinking of the letter. "Tell me about Jace. I don't remember him."

"He's not from here, but he's lived here awhile." Charlie pulled his brows together as if thinking back. "Five, maybe six years ago, he and his wife and their little girl moved here. That's his daughter with him. His parents bought the Revere Farm Brewery out on the highway."

"Revere went bankrupt."

"It did. Poor management and a host of other factors." Charlie's gaze slid to where Jace spoke with Mackenna before returning to Hannah. "They reopened the place as Skyline Farm Brewery. Jace and his father are the brewmasters. His mother runs the events."

"What about Jace's wife?"

"I heard she didn't like it here." Charlie shrugged. "They're divorced now and share custody of their daughter, whose name escapes me."

Hannah noticed Mackenna talking animatedly to Jace and his child. "Do you think he likes Mackenna?"

"I don't know." Charlie turned. "Here they come."

Mackenna's smile flashed bright and hot. "Hannah, I'd like to introduce you to some friends. This is Jace and Scarlett. Jace's parents own Skyline Farm Brewery, and he works there as a brewmaster."

"It's nice to meet you both." To Jace, Hannah added, "I'm eager to see what changes you and your family have made at the brewery."

Jace, tall and lean with a mop of brown hair and warm brown eyes, reached into his pocket and held out a couple of tickets to Hannah. "Come tonight, and you can see."

Hannah studied the tickets, then glanced up. "Blues, Brews and Barbecue?"

"We have blues artist Big John Walker performing. Some of our latest IPAs will be offered, and several food trucks will be there to provide amazing barbecue."

"I'll definitely be there." Mackenna shot Jace a sunny smile. "I already have my ticket."

Hannah stared down at the two tickets in her hand and cast a questioning glance at Charlie.

They bypassed the stage area and food trucks and headed straight for the barn. The doors to the structure were open wide with a constant flow of patrons in and out.

"The barn was in poor repair when Jace and his family took over. Instead of building new, they had a structural engineer come out and look it over." Admiration filled Charlie's eyes. "It's good to see it regain its former glory."

While the outside was pretty, with all that yellow paint and white trim, the inside was striking. Large windows cut into the back wall flooded the area with natural light. The floor, now a glossy hardwood, shone as if it had been freshly polished that morning.

Along the walls on this level, booths had been set up, offering everything from IPA beer gift packs to craft-a-brew kits and T-shirts.

As each booth appeared to be experiencing a surge of business, Hannah and Charlie returned to the bright sunshine.

Hannah thought how Lisa would have enjoyed the activity and festive atmosphere. "I'm sorry your mother couldn't join us tonight."

"If she hadn't already had plans with friends, she'd be here. She takes advantage of every opportunity to socialize." Satisfaction filled Charlie's voice. "My mom is not about to let MS define her. She finds a way to do what she wants and isn't too proud to ask for help when she needs it."

"She's a remarkable woman." Hannah thought of the other patients and families she'd met while Brian was going through treatment. "Everyone responds differently when life takes a hard turn."

"Brian appeared to handle it well. Each time we spoke, he was upbeat and positive." Charlie paused. "Unless that was what he wanted to convey?"

Hannah hesitated.

Charlie immediately held up his hands. "Forget it. That's personal."

"You were his best friend, Charlie," Hannah reminded him. "If you don't have a right to know, I'm not sure who would."

"Though we spoke frequently on the phone, I only made it up there once after his diagnosis." Charlie's eyes turned dark with memories. "It was still early days, and he had that 'I'm going to fight and win this battle' mentality."

Hannah recalled that day. Brian had still been good enough to be home alone, and she'd been at work. By the time she'd arrived home, Charlie had left to return to GraceTown.

"The diagnosis came as a complete shock to both of us. Brian had always been so healthy, and he took such good care of himself."

"A lot better than I do," Charlie agreed.

"A lot better than I do, too." Hannah expelled a breath. "Do you know that the first question everyone asked when they found out he had lung cancer was if he smoked? He never did, but what if he *had*?" Hannah ran a shaky hand through her hair. "I'm sorry. It upsets me to remember how those questions added stress to an already stressful time."

"It had to be difficult for you."

"It was worse for him," she said simply.

Charlie's gaze grew thoughtful. "I know your father came up a few times. I assume Brian's parents did, too."

"They stopped in frequently to visit." Hannah kept her voice even. "It was difficult for them and for Brian. He had his pride. As he got worse, he didn't want to see anyone. He said he didn't want them to remember him that way."

Then, afraid that sounded critical, she added, "I encouraged him to at least let his sister and parents visit."

*Enough talk about illness and death,* Hannah thought. She opened her mouth to suggest they sit and enjoy a beer when Charlie lifted a hand.

"Mr. Jessup." Charlie's greeting, warm and friendly, had the grizzled old man responding with an answering grin.

"Well, if it isn't Charlie Rogan." Merle Jessup turned to Hannah and grinned. "What's a pretty woman like you doing with this scallywag?"

Hannah didn't think she'd ever heard that term spoken outside of old pirate movies. But hearing it coming from a man whose face boasted deep lines and bristly silver and black whiskers somehow fit.

"I don't believe we've met." Hannah extended her hand. "Hannah Danbury."

"Danbury?" Merle rubbed his chin. "Any relation to Brian?"

"He was my husband."

"Was?" Merle's brows, full and bushy, winged up. "You two divorced?"

"Brian passed away last year," Hannah told him.

"I'm sorry to hear that. Brian was a good kid. Even if this one," Merle jerked a thumb in Charlie's direction, "led him into temptation on a daily basis."

Underlying the harsh sentiment, Hannah heard affection.

"Hey," Charlie protested. "What did I do?"

"Brought him onto my property." Merle's eyes appeared to glitter in the bright light. "Went swimming in Devil's Bathtub even though the area has more No Trespassing signs than the Clearance signs you see at Walmart."

"How do you know that it wasn't Brian leading me astray?" Charlie asked, neither confirming nor denying the trespassing.

"You were always the leader—" Merle began.

"That's not true." Hannah wasn't sure where the words came from, but she couldn't stop them. "My husband was a leader. He would never let anyone push him to do anything."

"He listened to this one." Merle expelled an exaggerated breath. "Don't ask me why."

her driveway, he put a hand on her arm to keep her from jumping out.

"Look, if you don't want to go to Devil's Bathtub with me, I understand, but don't go alone. Call Mackenna or someone else, just to be safe."

# CHAPTER ELEVEN

Hannah did call someone, but it wasn't Mackenna, and she wasn't sure if she was safe.

She stared down into the swirling water of Devil's Bathtub.

"We don't have to do this if you don't want to." Charlie's voice sounded in her ear.

Did she want to? Three days ago, she hadn't. This wasn't her kind of thing. Besides, it felt wrong to be doing this with Charlie instead of Brian.

Hannah had nearly put this off, then she'd read the letter again. This was one of the places where Brian had been the happiest, a place he'd wanted to share with her.

But Brian wasn't here to go with her, so if she was going to try to honor him, this was the best way.

"The water is deep." Charlie stood beside her, close but not touching. "It's difficult to tell from up here, but there's no worry about hitting the bottom when you jump."

Surrounded by smooth stone, the "bathtub," sported clear water the color of aquamarine. The pool of water flowed into a river that eventually culminated in a small waterfall.

"I'm doing this." Stripping off her shorts to reveal a modest black one-piece, Hannah jumped. The rush that accompanied the quick drop into the water didn't prepare her for the thrill of plunging deep into the clear, cold water.

She grinned, understanding why Brian had thought this was fun.

Treading water, Hannah called out to Charlie, "Come on in. The water is amazing."

Grinning, Charlie pulled off his shirt, revealing a broad, muscular chest with a smattering of dark hair that arrowed down into his swim trunks.

He motioned her to the side with one hand. "Out of the way. I don't want to land on you."

She swam to the side of Devil's Bathtub, her fingers finding purchase on a smooth edge. Gazing up, she taunted, "What are you waiting for?"

The force of him hitting the water sent the waves churning. In seconds, he surfaced, a big grin on his face, his hair dripping water. "You were right. The water is amazing."

"A bit cold," she admitted, her teeth chattering.

"A little." When he smiled at her, everything in her went warm.

"What did you guys do after you jumped?"

"We tried to push the other under the water." Charlie leaned back and floated.

"You did not."

"We did."

"Like this." Hannah spanned the short distance between them and pushed hard on his stomach. Which was rock-hard. He barely moved from the force of her shove, but his head did go partially under.

He came up sputtering, with a devilish gleam in his eyes. "Is that how you want to play it?"

"My meager attempt to re-create fun times." She grinned at him, then shrieked when he moved to her, put his hands on her shoulders and pushed her under.

She didn't go alone.

He came with her.

Her gaze locked with his for an instant before they both returned to the surface.

"Well, that was fun."

Charlie grinned. "I think the dunking-and-pushing lends itself more to boys."

This time, it was Hannah who leaned back and floated. "Probably right. I like this better. Warm sun. Cool water. Blue sky."

When Charlie swam near, she worried for a second that he planned to dunk her again. Instead, he floated beside her, his gaze focused on the sky, his hand resting on the water so close she needed only to reach out to curl her fingers around his.

Her hand seemed to move of its own accord. Her fingers did no more than brush his before he took her hand lightly in his.

There was comfort in the touch, in the feel of not being utterly alone, which was how she'd felt for most of the past year.

As they floated, Hannah totally relaxed and let all worries slip away.

She wasn't sure how long they floated in silence. A rustling sound pulled her attention from the sky. A large buck gazed down at them from the spot where she and Charlie had jumped.

He studied them for several heartbeats, then turned and walked away.

"Did you see that?" Hannah asked, giving up the floating to tread water.

Charlie smiled. "There are lots of them in this area. I don't recall ever seeing one this close to the edge."

"I'm glad he didn't jump." Hannah shivered, envisioning three hundred pounds of deer hitting the water.

"They're smarter than that." Charlie glanced up. "Clouds are moving in. It appears the storm predicted for tomorrow is going to arrive sooner than forecast. We should probably head for the truck."

Hannah knew once they got out of the water, once this magical time came to an end, words wouldn't come as easily.

She reached over and touched Charlie's arm for a second. "We should go. But first I want to thank you for bringing me here. It's a happy place."

"You feel close to Brian here."

Hannah hesitated, then nodded. There was no reason to tell Charlie that right now the one she felt closest to in this place was him.

Charlie stepped out the garage, thankful he'd gotten his truck inside before the rain started. The deluge that appeared on its way hadn't yet arrived, but from the looks of the thunderheads, it wouldn't be long.

"Thanks again for this afternoon." Hannah reached out as if to touch his arm, but pulled back.

She might have simply been gesturing. She talked with her hands a lot. He certainly didn't want to read something into nothing.

Like when they'd linked hands while floating. That had definitely felt like something, a connection between him and her. Then again, he could be dead wrong about that, too.

"Do you and your mom have plans for dinner?"

Charlie blinked. "What?"

"Dinner plans? I've got a pan of lasagna in the freezer. I'd have to bring it over since I have no furniture in my dining room, unless you don't mind eating in the kitchen?"

"I'm sure my mom would appreciate the offer, but she's at a card club this afternoon, and they have dinner together afterwards. As far as me eating in the kitchen, that's not a problem."

Hannah glanced up at the distant rumble of thunder. "Won't she come home early to avoid driving in the weather?"

"Her friend Penny picked her up. If the weather gets bad, they'll wait until it clears."

"What if it doesn't clear for a while?"

"It'll lighten up at some point. If Penny doesn't want to drive, I'll go pick Mom up. It's not far."

"What about you?"

"I don't mind driving in rain."

"No." Hannah licked her lips. "About dinner. Are you interested?"

He locked his gaze on hers. "I am interested."

Time seemed to stretch, and something passed between them, a feeling that surprised Charlie with its intensity.

"When do you want me to come over?" he asked, breaking the silence.

"Now?"

"Let me grab a quick shower and put on clean clothes." He smiled. "Then I'll be over."

Another rumble of thunder sounded, this one closer.

Her lips quirked up in a smile. "Come around back, and don't take too long, or you'll be getting a second shower on the way over."

By the time Hannah had showered and dressed, thunder rumbled overhead more frequently, and rain sputtered from a rapidly darkening sky.

A knock on the back door sounded just as the gentle pitter-patter became a torrent.

Opening the door, she motioned Charlie inside and hurriedly shut the door behind him. "That was close."

He reached up and rubbed the ends of her still-damp hair

between his fingers, his knuckles grazing her cheek. "Looks like I'm not the only one who got wet."

Air suddenly seemed in short supply. When she found enough to speak, she sounded breathless. "A shower seemed like a good idea."

Charlie didn't appear to notice her breathlessness. He sniffed the air. "I don't smell lasagna."

"I haven't put it in yet." She gestured to the stove, where the casserole dish waited on top. "Though it's ready to go, and I have the oven preheated."

While he watched, she stuck the pan into the oven and set the timer. By the time she straightened, he was no longer beside her. Instead, he stood in the entrance to the dining room, studying the hardwood floor.

Apparently hearing her approach, he pointed to the floor without shifting his gaze. "Looks amazing."

"You were right. Sparks & Son does excellent work." Hannah smiled. "Thanks again for referring Harley."

He finally turned toward her. "I'm surprised they got on it so quickly."

Hannah shrugged. "Apparently, they had another job that fell through. My lucky day. They'll be out again tomorrow to give it another coat."

"Where did you put the furniture?"

"It's gone."

Charlie arched an eyebrow.

"I donated it all. I didn't like it, so why keep it around?"

"A decisive woman. Good for you."

She turned toward the kitchen, then back to him. "If you don't mind chopping vegetables, you can help me with the salad."

"Chopping? Knives?" He grinned. "Bring on the fun."

When he sat at the small dinette table that had seen better decades and began to chop with great gusto, Hannah turned her attention to the homemade yeast rolls in the breadbasket.

"This is my special seasoning blend," she told Charlie, the shaker poised above the rolls. "If you don't like garlic, I can leave it off yours."

"I love garlic." He shot her a wink. "You'll discover, if you're around me any time at all, that I like almost everything."

"I'm like that, too," she told him. "But some of my friends have very specific likes and dislikes, so I always ask."

While she spun the salad, her gaze drifted out the window. Though there should still be some daylight, the storm had made it nearly pitch-black outside.

Even as lightning lit up the sky and rain slapped the windows, the scent of spice, meat and cheese filled the kitchen.

"Smells amazing." As Charlie inhaled deeply, his stomach growled. He offered a sheepish grin. "I didn't eat much for lunch, and I built up quite an appetite attacking the vegetables."

She rolled her eyes. When they shared a smile, everything inside her went warm. "If you like, we could start with salads and rolls. The lasagna will be done in forty minutes."

"That works." Charlie glanced around. "What else can I do to help?"

"There are several salad dressings in the refrigerator. I like the balsamic vinaigrette, so if you wouldn't mind, could you grab that one and whatever you want for yourself?"

Once he'd done that and she set the salad bowls and plate of rolls on the dinette table, Hannah had to chuckle. "My dad called this eating in shifts. Let me say he wasn't a fan."

Charlie made a great show of glancing around as he sat down again. "I don't believe I see your father."

Hannah grinned, then lifted a hand and brought it down as if waving a starting flag. "Let the first shift begin."

They ate salad and rolls, then moved on to the lasagna once it was ready.

Instead of awkward, their dinner at the pocket-sized table in her small kitchen felt comfortably cozy. Probably because there was nothing flirtatious in his manner. If there had been, she'd have shut it down.

Well, she was almost positive she'd have shut him down.

"To me, there's nothing better than this." Charlie gestured with one hand. "Amazing food, fabulous wine and interesting conversation."

"Don't forget, we're also dry." The words had barely left her lips when the wind pushed a sheet of rain against the window.

Though Hannah wasn't a bit cold, she shivered. It was odd how the bright and sunny morning had so quickly turned dark and foreboding.

It reminded her, in many ways, of her life. Hannah recalled vividly those early years with Brian that had brimmed to over-flowing with light and promise. One trip to the ER had brought the darkness. Only now was the light beginning to shine again.

Charlie forked off a bite of lasagna. "Since we're now eating the entrée, would your dad call this the second shift or the main course?"

Hannah only chuckled. "I spoke with him today."

"How's he liking Florida?"

"Better than I thought he would, considering he doesn't like change." Hannah took a sip of wine. "I hope Sandie loves the furniture they purchased, because she'll likely be stuck with those pieces the rest of her life."

Charlie twirled the stem of his wineglass back and forth between his fingers. "I recall Leon wasn't much for change, especially not once he had what he considered the right item in the right space, but he and Sandie are still young. Furniture wears out. And hey, sometimes you just want to change things up."

"Perhaps he'll be different with Sandie. I hope so." Hannah picked up her fork, but only moved the lasagna around on her plate. "Growing up, whenever I wanted to move around the furniture in my room, he wouldn't let me. He insisted the layout was perfect just the way it was."

Charlie pointed his fork at her. "It may have taken a decade, but you eventually got your way."

Hannah cocked her head, not understanding.

"You moved in and got rid of it all."

"I guess that's one way to look at it." Hannah laughed and glanced out the window, pleased to see the rain was letting up. "Small changes are easy for me. Big changes are sometimes more difficult. I find myself second-guessing my decisions."

"Still, you make them." Charlie took a contemplative sip of wine and studied her over the rim. "Got any big ones you're considering now?"

Hannah hesitated, then reminded herself that if anyone would understand forging your own path, it would be the man sitting across from her.

"Instead of getting a job at the college in the fall, where I'd have good pay and benefits, I'm thinking I might want to work in a bakery." Simply thinking of inhaling the tantalizing scents of yeast, cinnamon and powdered sugar all day made her smile. "I love everything about baking. I especially enjoy experimenting with ingredients."

"Like the cupcakes you brought over for us?"

"Yes, like those." Hannah sat back in her chair, her spirits buoyed by the fact that the rain had finally ceased, and a ray of sunlight now streamed through the window. Or maybe it was the spark of interest in Charlie's eyes.

"Those were incredible."

The heartfelt compliment had blood rushing through her veins like warm honey. "That experiment worked. Others, well, not all are successes."

"Hey, Edison failed ten thousand times before he perfected the first modern electric lamp."

Hannah inclined her head. "Is that really meant to be encouraging?"

Charlie's easy smile reached his eyes. "Why a bakery? From

what I understand, bakers start work at three a.m., or some other equally crazy hour."

"I'm talking about working the counter. It'd give me an opportunity to meet lots of new people. You know, reconnect with the community. I'd also be able to observe firsthand how a bakery operates."

The interest in Charlie's eyes now shone even more brightly. "Are you thinking of eventually going into business for yourself?"

"I am." The thought had been rolling around in Hannah's mind, but being her father's daughter, she was cautious. "I'm gathering information and exploring options. I'm considering specialty cakes, like for weddings and birthdays, with cupcakes on the side. I don't know exactly how my business would look. What I do know is, whatever I do, I want to be happy."

A slow smile spread across Charlie's face. "A worthy goal."

"You don't think I'm being foolish?"

"How can spending your time focusing on something you love ever be foolish?"

# CHAPTER TWELVE

Charlie helped Hannah clear the table and load the dishwasher. He moved slowly, sensing the evening was coming to a close. Though they'd spent hours together, he still wasn't ready for their time together to end.

"Looks like the rain has finally moved out of the area," Hannah observed, shutting the dishwasher.

Though Charlie had a perfect view from where he was standing, he moved beside her and peered out the window. "Did Brian ever tell you about how we used to sneak out at night to go camping when we were in high school?"

Hannah swiveled, which brought her so close he could see the flecks of gold in her eyes and smell the enticing citrus scent of her shampoo.

She pushed a strand of hair back from her face and gave a nervous-sounding laugh. "That surprises me. Brian insisted on staying in four-star hotels whenever he traveled. He always said staying in low-end chain motels was like camping. The comment led me to conclude he didn't like camping."

As if thinking she'd said too much, Hannah clamped her lips together.

"Who doesn't prefer the luxury life?" Charlie resisted a sudden urge to slide his hand down her hair to see if it was as soft as it looked. "I don't know if he lost his taste for it or not. I only know he used to love life in the great outdoors."

Hannah's doubtful expression made him smile.

"It's true. Scout's honor." He twisted his fingers to form the Boy Scout salute. "In fact, in high school, we had this secret code for a camping trip. You know the tent emoji?"

"There's a tent emoji?" Hannah pulled out her phone, swiped a few times, then paused and held up her phone. "This one?"

"Yep." Just seeing the tiny tent on the screen had memories flooding back. "We used to sneak out during the night and camp in the woods. Brian's dad had these single-person tents that he called pup tents. He'd tossed them out, and I pulled them out of the trash and took them home."

"This story is getting more and more bizarre." Hannah rested her back against the counter and offered an encouraging smile.

Charlie remained where he was, liking the closeness. "If one of us texted the tent emoji during the night, it was code that we were up for a camping trip that night. If the other responded with a thumbs-up, we'd meet at my place in thirty minutes."

"Why your place?"

"There were several dogs in Brian's neighborhood that could be yappy." Charlie's lips curved as he remembered. "Plus, I had the tents. We were always home before dawn."

Hannah's eyes twinkled. "What would you do once you set up the tents?"

"Drink Mountain Dew, eat junk food and get very little sleep. It was a blast." Charlie expelled a breath. "Good times. Happy times."

"Isn't being in the woods at night dangerous?"

"Most everything in life carries an element of danger." Charlie shrugged. "On the whole, the woods are pretty safe."

A lot safer than standing next to his best friend's widow,

whom he suddenly wanted to kiss.

~

The next day, Hannah met Mackenna for lunch at Auggie and Arlo's, a bistro near the college. Spending time with her friend and hearing the happy chatter surrounding them buoyed Hannah's already sunny mood.

"I'm sorry about ditching you on Sunday," Mackenna said, two bright swaths of pink coloring her cheeks. "There's no excuse other than when I get around Jace, I sort of forget about anything else."

"It was okay." Hannah offered her friend a reassuring smile. "Charlie and I walked around for a little while, went to the brewery for a bit, then I went home."

"It won't happen again," Mackenna insisted. "Forgive me?"

"Already forgotten." Hannah waved a hand. "And forgiven."

"You and Charlie." Mackenna gazed at her, a half-smile on her lips, and stabbed a piece of endive. "I heard you had him over for dinner last night."

Though Hannah had been about to bring that up herself, it startled her that Mackenna already knew. "Who told you?"

"Sean O'Malley's wife works at the college. Tawdra and I were walking in from the parking lot at the same time this morning. She mentioned it."

"How did Tawdra know?" Hannah pulled her brows together. "They live down the block, and Charlie is next door to me."

"Nothing goes on in that neighborhood without Beverly and Geraldine knowing about it." Mackenna dipped her fork into her dressing and stabbed more lettuce. "One of them told Tawdra. Is it true?"

"It's not a big deal." Hannah took a bite of her sandwich. The bistro was known for its turkey Reubens, and she hadn't had one in years. "We went out to Devil's Bathtub that afternoon, and when we got back, I offered to make dinner as a token of my appreciation for him arranging the excursion with Mr. Jessup."

"Are you and Charlie dating?" Mackenna didn't bother to modulate her voice, and two women at a nearby table turned.

The likelihood that they knew Charlie, or even knew which Charlie was being discussed, was small. Still, Hannah flushed.

Leaning forward, Hannah lowered her voice. "Charlie was just helping me out by taking me to the place Brian mentioned in his letter."

"That's right." Mackenna's brown eyes sparkled. "The mysterious letter you got from the old woman in the forest. The one from Brian, even though he's been gone a year."

"I know it sounds crazy." Hannah kept a firm grip on her rising emotions at her friend's flippant tone. "But the letter was in Brian's handwriting, and Charlie said the places that were mentioned are places the two of them used to visit."

"I still don't understand why you went to Devil's Bathtub." Mackenna's tone turned puzzled. "Brian simply said he wished you and he had been together back then so you could have enjoyed going there with him."

"That's what the letter said." Hannah took another bite of the Reuben, but found she'd lost her appetite.

"So why go there with Charlie?" Mackenna reminded Hannah of a dog with a bone. For some unknown reason, she wouldn't let the subject drop. "I mean, it isn't as if Brian gave you a bucket list."

"You're right. It isn't a bucket list." Hannah sat back in the booth. "But the fact that Brian listed three specific activities tells me they were important to him. I thought if I could go to Devil's Bathtub, maybe see what he saw, feel what he felt—"

"With Charlie."

This time, Hannah frowned. "Something is obviously on your mind. Instead of dancing around it, why don't you tell me what it is?"

Mackenna hesitated for a long moment, appearing to weigh her options. Options, which in Hannah's mind, were either denying or admitting that Hannah's suspicions were on target.

"You just got back into town. You're rebuilding your life here." Mackenna expelled a breath. "I don't know that you're ready to jump into a relationship, especially with a man who seems to avoid entanglements at all costs."

Hannah laughed out loud, the full, robust sound drawing head turns all around. She couldn't help it. Mackenna's fears were so off target, they were laughable.

"OMG, you really think there is something romantic going on between me and Charlie Rogan."

The bright spots of pink returned to Mackenna's cheeks. Back in high school, her friend had tended to blush. It appeared that hadn't changed.

Mackenna lifted her chin. "Why wouldn't I think that? You were at the street dance with him. You went to Blues, Brews and Barbecue with him. Now you're making dinner for him. What else am I to think?"

"Charlie is my neighbor. He was my husband's best friend and has been helping me get settled." Hannah's tone brooked no argument. "There's nothing the slightest bit romantic between the two of us."

When she got home from her lunch with Mackenna, Hannah put on her hiking boots and headed into the woods.

Instead of following a specific path, she wandered aimlessly, letting the sights and sounds of the forest wrap around her. On the needle-covered path, the scent of evergreen mingled with the smell of damp moss.

Pausing, Hannah leaned close to study a shrub with bright red berries. Winterberry?

"This is a nice surprise."

Hannah jerked upright. Her heart slammed against her rib cage.

Maisie stood close enough to touch, her blue eyes radiating warmth. Like her, the woman wore long pants, sturdy walking shoes and a simple cotton shirt.

*Two women enjoying an impromptu meeting in the woods.*

The realization that this meeting was nowhere near that simple made Hannah smile. She'd spent hours in these woods looking for Maisie and the pink house. Now, when she wasn't searching, the woman appeared. "I've been looking for you."

"Well, if you thought you'd find me in the winterberry," Maisie gestured, her tone teasing, "it's no wonder I had to come looking for you."

Hannah blinked. "You were looking for me? Why?"

"I was worried." Maisie's brow furrowed as her gaze searched Hannah's face. "I saw that receiving the letter upset you. I wanted to make sure you were okay."

First things first. She would not allow herself to be distracted this time. "How did you get the letter? There was no address on the envelope."

Maisie startled her by reaching out and giving Hannah's hand a squeeze. "Sometimes things come into our possession at exactly the right time."

Warmth flowed through Hannah's fingers and up her arm. The nervous beating of her heart quieted.

Maisie's tone was equally soothing when she said, "Do you want to tell me about the letter?"

Emotion had Hannah clearing her throat before responding. "It was from my husband, Brian. He wanted me to know there were so many things he'd have done differently if he'd known our time together would be so short."

"Let's walk." Maisie slipped her arm around Hannah's.

Hannah was about to say the path was too narrow for them to

stroll side by side, but then she saw that wasn't the case. An opening as wide as a bike trail lay before them.

"Regret is a funny thing." Maisie paused by a tree to sniff a cluster of maroon flowers. A smile curved her lips as she straightened. "The scent is heavenly."

Though Hannah wanted to push, impatient for Maisie to answer her questions, she thought of how she'd vowed to take time to appreciate not only the people in her life, but the beauty around her.

Bending close, she inhaled deeply, then glanced over at Maisie. "You're right. The fragrance is amazing."

Maisie offered an approving smile. "You're learning."

Hannah pushed the hair that had fallen forward back from her face and offered a tentative smile. "I don't understand."

"Regret encompasses so much. It can be about something we've done or, like with your husband, something left undone. Whatever the regret, I believe the benefit is in what it teaches us. Hopefully, we learn and move on, wiser than before."

"Brian wished he'd taken time to share with me some activities he'd done as a boy," Hannah confided.

Bolstered by Maisie's encouraging smile, Hannah continued. "They were such simple things—eating a snowball at the Frederick County Fair, fishing in Pigeon Creek and swimming in Devil's Bathtub."

"I haven't thought of Devil's Bathtub in years." Maisie chuckled. "Does Merle still have No Trespassing signs posted everywhere?"

Hannah smiled. "He does. But he let Charlie and me swim there."

Maisie arched a brow. "Charlie?"

"Charlie Rogan. He was Brian's best friend."

"Did you enjoy your swim?"

Hannah couldn't stop the smile. "I can't recall the last time I had so much fun."

"That doesn't surprise me. It's often the simplest things that give us the most pleasure." Maisie's expression turned wistful. "Like sitting in front of a roaring fire or enjoying a meal and conversation with a friend or someone you love."

An image of the lasagna she and Charlie had enjoyed had Hannah nodding. Then she refocused.

"What's strange is the activities Brian mentioned weren't ones I'd think he would particularly enjoy." Hannah felt her breath hitch. "I admit it made me wonder for a second if I knew my husband at all."

"People are constantly changing and growing." Though Maisie's hand didn't move, Hannah swore she felt Maisie stroke her arm. "That may be why teenage Brian liked things that you can't imagine the man you married doing. It's also why you often have little in common with those who were once your childhood friends, while those who weren't your friends growing up suit you now."

"I'm reaching out to some friends from high school and hoping to get together with them in the next few weeks." Hannah blew out a breath. "It's anyone's guess how that will go."

"You're putting yourself out there." Maisie's tone turned matter-of-fact. "If it works out, great. If not, you made the effort. No regrets."

"I never thought about it in those terms." Hannah stared curiously at her. "Thanks for the insight."

A pleased look blanketed Maisie's face.

"Imparting wisdom gained through experience is a…" Maisie paused. "It's my pleasure."

A comfortable silence descended, and Hannah was the first to break it. "Since the activities seemed important to Brian, I decided I would do them all. I hope they'll make me feel close to him."

"Did visiting Devil's Bathtub do that?"

Shaking her head, Hannah tried not to think of how close

she'd felt to Charlie. "I tried a snowball at the fair, too. I'm still deciding if I'll try fishing. Charlie also mentioned that he and Brian did a lot of camping."

"Embracing new experiences will allow you to stretch in directions that will help you get to know yourself better." Maisie's tone softened. "Take advantage of these opportunities. I didn't always do that, and like your husband, I discovered that life is fleeting, and time is a gift."

Hannah nodded. If the past two years had taught her anything, it was that life came with no guarantees. She cast a look around as she continued to stroll down the strange wide path with Maisie. "I can't tell you how many times I've searched these woods looking for you and the pink house."

"Well, it appears today is when we were meant to find each other again." Maisie inclined her head. "Tell me about Charlie. Have you and he always been close?"

"Close? Charlie and me?" The question startled Hannah, and she gave a little laugh. "Not at all. Back in high school, he was loud, always making jokes, always the center of attention."

Hannah realized with a start that she'd been jealous of how at home Charlie seemed in his own skin, jealous of how much everyone liked him.

A knowing look filled Maisie's blue eyes. "It sounds as if Charlie is one of those people who didn't suit you back in high school, but suits you now."

Something about the comment didn't sit right, but Hannah couldn't disagree. "Yes."

"I need to go now, but I promise we'll see each other again very soon." Before Hannah could say a word, Maisie turned and slipped between two bushy pines.

It took Hannah only a second to realize what was happening. Maisie was leaving. Leaving before she could tell Hannah how to find her and the pink house again. Leaving before she could explain how the envelope and letter had come into her possession.

Even as she pushed through the bristly branches and called out to Maisie, Hannah knew searching for the woman would be pointless.

Maisie had promised they'd see each other again, but it was obvious that their time for today had come to a close.

Twenty minutes later, Hannah burst out of the woods, eager to tell Charlie everything that had happened. When she spotted him in the driveway next to his truck, she picked up speed, running the last few feet.

Seconds before she reached Charlie, Hannah realized he wasn't alone. She skidded to a stop.

She'd been so focused on him that she hadn't noticed Hugh Quackenbush standing there. Her view of the widower, who'd lived in the neighborhood for as far back as Hannah could remember, had been partially blocked by Charlie's truck.

"Hannah." Hugh lifted a hand in greeting. "It's been a long time."

"It has. It's good to see you both." Hannah widened her smile to include Charlie, then gestured wide with one hand. "What a beautiful day this turned out to be."

"We need rain more than we need sunshine and blue skies." Hugh's lips pursed. "Rain was in the forecast again, but it went north this time."

"It happens." Hannah kept her tone light.

Now she recalled why she and her dad had never spent much time around Hugh. While there was a heart of gold under all that bluster, Hugh walked around under a dark cloud, complaining about everything.

"You're going to need to start watering your grass," Hugh told her. "Your bushes and trees need water, too. I noticed you have some webworm starting on the walnut in your backyard. Your father took excellent care of his lawn. I'd hate to see you let it go. A poorly maintained house and lawn affects everyone's property values."

"Thanks for the reminder." Hannah shifted her gaze to Charlie. "Stop over when you're done here?"

When he appeared to hesitate, she added, "If you have time, that is."

"I have time now." Charlie shot the older man a smile. "See you later, Hugh."

"Don't forget what I said about the walnut." Hugh pointed in the direction of her backyard. "Give those webworms an inch, and they'll take a mile."

"I'll get right on that," Hannah promised.

Charlie waited until they were out of earshot before speaking. "Thanks for rescuing me."

"Anytime."

Charlie's gaze searched her face, and his expression stilled. "What happened?"

"Let's sit, and I'll tell you." Hannah gestured to the swing. When she took a seat, Charlie dropped down beside her, leaving enough room so he could shift to face her.

When she didn't immediately start talking, worry clouded his dark eyes. "Are you okay?"

She tried for cool and calm, but her voice shook with excitement. "I had a conversation with Maisie this afternoon."

Charlie grinned. "You found the pink house again."

"Not the house. Just Maisie. I went for a walk in the woods, and she came up to me."

"She just walked up to you?"

"Yes." Hannah couldn't stop the smile, didn't even try. "She said she had come looking for me. She was worried."

"About?"

"She worried the letter had upset me."

"What did you tell her?"

*Everything.* Thinking about all that she had told a virtual stranger had Hannah inwardly shaking her head. The crazy thing was, Maisie didn't seem like a stranger.

"I told her it didn't upset me. That I was glad she gave it to me."

His gaze searched her face. "Did she tell you where she got it?"

"She gave me another cryptic reply." For some reason, knowing how Maisie had gotten the letter didn't seem as important to Hannah as seeing her again.

"What did you talk about?" Charlie pressed.

"Regrets." Hannah remembered every word of the conversation. "Over things not done or left undone."

Charlie offered an encouraging smile.

"We discussed learning from past regrets and simple things giving us pleasure."

That familiar easy smile lifted his lips. "Like lasagna and wine on a rainy afternoon?"

The fact that his mind had gone immediately in the same direction as hers gave Hannah pause, but she nodded. "I also admitted that I couldn't picture Brian enjoying the activities he'd looked back on with such fondness."

Charlie didn't, as she thought he might, try to convince her otherwise. "What did she say to that?"

"That people are always changing and growing. That who we were as teenagers isn't who we are now."

"Sounds like a heavy discussion."

"It didn't feel heavy," Hannah insisted. "It was nice. Like two friends talking. She said we were meant to find each other. I believe that."

"Do you think you'll see her again?"

"Oh, I'll definitely see her again." Hannah blew out a breath. "The question is when."

# CHAPTER THIRTEEN

That night, as Hannah lay in bed, the conversation she'd had with Maisie about regrets over things not done ran through her head.

She'd never been impulsive. But during the past year, she had done her best to open herself up to new experiences without overthinking it.

Could she be the kind of person to simply decide on a whim to spend the night in the woods? No planning, no organizing, just send a text and go for it?

Rolling over, she grabbed her phone from the bedside stand and texted Charlie.

His reply to her tent emoji arrived seconds later. Thumbs-up.

Twenty minutes later, Hannah strode out of the house. Dressed in jeans and a long-sleeved tee, she carried only a lightweight sleeping bag she'd found in the back of one of her dad's closets and a backpack.

Charlie stood in his driveway, the tents slung over his shoulder. He grinned when he saw her. "Can I interest you in an adventure?"

Hannah chuckled and simply began walking toward the woods. Charlie fell into step beside her. Though the woods loomed dark and mysterious ahead, all Hannah felt was excitement.

"Seeing the tent emoji pop up on my screen gave me a déjà vu moment." Charlie paused when they reached the edge of the woods. "Brian and I had our favorite spot. We can go there or—"

"That'll be fine." Hannah really didn't want to traipse through the woods in the dark, looking for a place to camp.

Charlie bumped her backpack with his elbow. "What do you have in here?"

"Snacks."

In the glow of the moon, she saw interest spark in his dark eyes. "What kind?"

"You'll have to wait to find out."

Twenty minutes later, Charlie grinned and popped a cake ball into his mouth. "The Twizzlers and Oreos I brought are good. These are better."

Hannah sipped a Diet Coke. "Cake balls are hard to beat."

She leaned back against a tree. Once they'd gotten to the spot where Charlie and Brian used to camp, they'd cleared it enough to set up the two tents.

Since it wasn't cold and they didn't plan to cook, they didn't bother with a fire. Instead, once the chores were done, they lit Charlie's lantern and dug into the snacks.

"You do this so well." Charlie studied the small pink cake ball —his second—before taking a bite.

The ball, devil's food covered in a pink shell of frosting with white sprinkles and topped with a chocolate bow, had his eyes closing for a second and a moan of pleasure escaping his lips.

"That one is gluten-free."

Surprise skittered across his face. "It tastes good."

"Gluten-free doesn't have to taste bad." To illustrate, Hannah took a big bite out of the one in her hand.

Charlie reached for another. "Tell me how you make these."

As she explained, Hannah realized that Charlie was a good

listener. It didn't hit her that she was doing most of the talking until she paused to take a breath.

Well, she could be a good listener, too. And she had lots of questions. When she and Mackenna had had lunch, her friend had mentioned Charlie made stuff in his garage. Hannah was embarrassed to admit that while she knew he was an entrepreneur, that's about all she knew.

Charlie wiped his fingers on one of the paper napkins she'd brought. "You could totally make money off these."

"I appreciate the vote of confidence. Enough about me." Hannah waved a dismissive hand. "Let's talk about you for a change. I've been dying to know what you do for a living."

Considering the amount of time they'd spent together, not knowing seemed rather pathetic.

"What if I prefer to remain dark and mysterious?"

"You couldn't pull off dark and mysterious if you tried."

He put a hand to his chest. "You wound me with your sharp words."

Hannah wanted to laugh, but wouldn't give him the satisfaction. "For the record, I don't think acting is your forte either."

Charlie expelled a melodramatic sigh. "Since I can't wow you with my banter, I guess I'm going to have to amaze you with my shop tales."

This time, Hannah didn't hold back the laugh.

With exaggerated movements, Charlie snagged another cake ball from the container. He tossed it into his mouth, then picked up his can of Mountain Dew and washed it down. "Okay. I'm ready. Let the interrogation begin."

Hannah rolled her eyes. Charlie was so easy to be around and so much, well, fun.

"Let's go back to why you left MIT without graduating." Hannah wasn't certain why she was suddenly so curious about everything to do with Charlie Rogan, but this piece of his history had always puzzled her.

"I considered staying and finishing out my last two years. The coursework wasn't difficult, and I had a full ride. But my mother had been diagnosed with MS and was struggling. My dad, well, some people step up during hard times. Some don't."

Sympathy rose inside Hannah. "You came back to support your mother."

"Yes, but I was also bored in school. I was eager to work on my own designs. In my own time. In my own way." Charlie's expression turned serious. "The building out back is my studio, or my workshop—either term fits. I have an office out there as well as equipment for testing designs."

"What exactly do you design?"

She listened as he took her through the capabilities of his first major success, a new and improved launch scan tool widely used by mechanics.

"The tool is sturdy and works with most brands of cars. It has a wide range of capabilities, including accessing and controlling modules, along with data reading and graphing."

He veered into the technical and lost her.

Did Charlie know that his eyes snapped with excitement when he spoke of vehicle control module specifications and mobile intelligent terminals? Or how the words tumbled out when he relayed the particulars regarding patents?

Brian, she realized, had been right. Charlie was one brilliant guy.

"How do you make money off your designs?" Hannah pulled her brows together. "I mean it's not as if you have a manufacturing plant making these tools."

"I licensed the patent with one of the top manufacturers of automotive tools." Charlie's tone remained matter-of-fact. "The monthly royalty payments allow me to continue to work on my other projects. I love being on my own. No office politics. Or, if there are any, they're with myself."

Hannah rolled her eyes. "You're hilarious. Ever consider

doing stand-up?"

"Thanks for the suggestion." He lifted his can of Mountain Dew. "I may give it a try if this design gig goes dry."

"If I'm hearing you right," she took a sip of soda, her gaze firmly fixed on his face, "a normal workday consists of planning and working out the kinks of your next latest-and-greatest."

"A bit simplistic, but accurate." He smiled. "The kinks are what takes time."

"What you do…" She paused, trying to think of the right way to say this. "It isn't confined to the hours of nine to five."

Though it had initially appeared to Hannah that Charlie spent very little time working, she now realized he had no constraints. He could create late at night or early in the morning.

"It's also not a straight line. Often—frequently—an idea needs to percolate. Sometimes I take fifty wrong turns before I find success. And that specific success may be only a small part of the larger project."

Hannah idly picked up another cake ball. Was this her second or third? Did it even matter?

She closed her mouth around it and found him staring. Her lips tingled, and swaths of heat warmed her cheeks. "Go on. I'm listening."

"I work best without pressure, especially the kind of pressure exerted by someone focused on the bottom line. And because I genuinely enjoy what I do, it doesn't feel like work to me."

Hannah nodded. She understood this mentality far better than he realized.

"I don't know if you remember my dad," he said.

"I don't think I ever met him." She'd remembered his mother only because of knowing her through her job at the library.

"He worked at Siegrist. He was a tool-and-die man."

Hannah brought her memory of the business into focus. "Siegrist is the place out on the highway."

"That's right. He worked there from the time he got out of

community college until he left GraceTown." For the first time that evening, the sparkle left Charlie's eyes. "He complained about his job nonstop."

"Why did he stay all those years if he hated it so much?"

Charlie shrugged. "Even as a kid, I remember thinking that when I grew up, that wasn't going to be my life."

Hannah recalled Brian telling her that Tom Rogan had left his job and GraceTown even before his divorce from Lisa was final. "What's he doing now?"

"Don't know. Don't care."

"Because of the divorce?"

"Because he walked away from my mother when she was in the hospital and needed him most. He never looked back." Charlie's eyes went flat and hard.

Hannah swallowed against the lump in her throat. "I'm sorry I made you remember."

"Just because you don't talk about something doesn't mean you don't remember."

"You're right." Just because Hannah didn't bring Brian up all the time anymore didn't mean he wasn't on her mind. "I am sorry he was such a disappointment to you and your mom."

"When he married her, he vowed he'd be there in sickness and in health. I guess he had a short memory." Charlie's tone turned fierce. "I would never walk away like that."

Hannah shook her head. "No. You're not that kind of person."

"You're not that kind either." Charlie surprised her by reaching over and covering her hand with his. "You were there for Brian when he needed you most."

"I did my best." Hannah expelled a breath. "When Brian got sick, well, I didn't know what to say, and whatever I did say, it was usually wrong."

"I don't believe that." Charlie's fingers tightened around her hand.

"You weren't there. You don't know." Only then did Hannah

realize how cold her fingers were, a coldness that went all the way to her bones as she recalled those brief weeks between Brian's diagnosis and his death.

"Why don't you give me an example?" Charlie's voice, low and calm, encouraged confidences. "Let me be the judge."

Hannah shifted her gaze over his left shoulder and spoke into the darkness. "The prognosis was poor from the beginning. While the doctors did offer a few options, they weren't optimistic. I tried to be positive, to, you know, be his cheerleader. The whole 'you're going to do great,' 'you're strong and determined.' I shied away from mentioning anything negative. It didn't feel like the right approach."

His hand still covered hers, and she made no move to pull away, finding comfort in the simple touch.

"Brian wanted to be realistic."

"I tried that route, too." Hannah's tone turned bleak. "I'd tell him I was going to miss him so much and how my life wouldn't be the same without him."

"He didn't want to hear that either."

Hannah slowly shook her head and pulled her attention back to Charlie. "He would get so angry, asking why I had him already buried when he was still fighting to live." Tears filled her eyes. "I didn't have him dead and buried. I just wanted to make sure he knew how much I loved him."

The tears spilled over and slipped down her cheeks.

"You didn't do anything wrong." Leaning over, Charlie cupped her face in his large hands, his eyes dark and intense. "It was a difficult time for him and for you. You were both doing the best you could under horrible circumstances. The love you shared is what matters."

Hannah didn't know what to say, wasn't sure she could have found her voice even if she'd had something to say.

"Brian loved you, Hannah. With his whole heart. And you loved him. If you remember nothing else, remember that."

# CHAPTER FOURTEEN

Hannah crawled into her pup tent and wiggled into the sleeping bag, conscious of Charlie's protective gaze on her. After too many cake balls, coupled with a can of soda with caffeine, Hannah worried she might not be able to sleep when they finally called it a night.

Despite the hard ground beneath her and the caffeine and sugar surging through her system, she fell asleep immediately. She wasn't sure what caused her to wake several hours later.

Or why, instead of lying there and drifting back to sleep, she unzipped the sleeping bag and crawled out of the tent.

The night air, warm and still, wrapped around her like a comfortable blanket as her eyes adjusted to the darkness. She sniffed the air.

Lily of the valley? Could the sweet scent be what had awakened her?

Hannah pulled her brows together in puzzlement. There were no plants in this immediate area. If there had been, she'd have noticed when they set up camp.

She took only a few steps forward before the moon came out

from behind the clouds. Her heart gave an excited leap as she spotted a swath of pink between two trees in the distance. Could she and Charlie have camped so close to the pink house and not even known it?

Hannah glanced at the tent where Charlie slept and considered waking him. She hesitated. What if it wasn't the pink house? What if it was simply some kind of weird reflection in the moonlight that produced the rosy glow? She'd have awakened him for nothing.

Turning on the flashlight on her phone, Hannah decided to go just a little farther and check it out. If it was the house, she'd return for Charlie.

She wove her way carefully through the trees and brush in the direction where she'd seen the pink. After a few steps, she heard a rustling in the nearby brush. The hair on her neck rose, and she whirled.

When she saw the green eyes, she realized she wasn't alone.

The scream jerked Charlie wide awake. His breath came fast as he shoved aside the sleeping bag and pushed out of the tent. His gaze swept the campsite, focusing immediately on Hannah's tent.

Empty.

Adrenaline surged. Fear had bile rising, and urgency filled his deep voice when he called out, "Hannah! Where are you?"

Without waiting for an answer, Charlie started off in the direction of the scream, fearing there might not be a second to waste.

"Over here." Her voice rose, high-pitched, then broke. "I'm over here. Please help me."

Altering his course, Charlie barreled through the brush. He found her with her back against a tree, her breath coming in short puffs.

"What's wrong?"

Grabbing his arm in a death grip, she pulled him to her and pointed. When she spoke, her voice was barely above a whisper. "Don't move. I think if you do, they'll pounce."

Green eyes stared unblinkingly at the two of them from the hollow of a tree. Charlie's breath came out on a whoosh. He nearly chuckled, the impulse born of relief. For Hannah's sake, he stifled the sound, knowing her fear was real.

He understood. The first time he'd come up against one of these creatures, he'd been nine, and the encounter had shaken him.

"It's a fisher-cat." Wrapping one arm around her shoulders, he spoke in a low tone intended to soothe. "They're nocturnal and live in these woods. He won't hurt you."

Her entire body trembled, and when he took her in his arms, she burrowed against him and spoke to the front of his sweatshirt. "I was going down that path when I saw him. I froze. Then I screamed."

"The way their green eyes glow in the dark is kind of creepy. I know the first time I ran across one at night, it spooked me." Charlie ran a hand down her hair and discovered it really was as soft as it looked. "I learned later that they're really quite timid."

Hannah gazed in the direction of the tree. Her eyes widened as she looked up at him. "It's gone."

"Like I said, they're shy creatures." He loosened his hold, but was pleased when she showed no inclination to step away. "What were you doing out here anyway?"

She cast another quick glance at the tree. Expelling a shuddering breath, she sagged against him, resting her head against his heart. "I woke up and thought I smelled lily of the valley. It's such a distinctive fragrance."

Charlie nodded, liking the way she fit so perfectly against him. She didn't seem in any hurry to tell her story, and he wasn't inclined to rush her. Not with her so soft and warm in his arms.

"I hadn't seen any plants when we put up our tent, but I got up, and when I was looking around, that's when I saw it."

"The green eyes?"

She jerked her head back, clipping his jaw.

"I'm sorry." She offered a wan smile. "No, the green eyes came later."

"What came first?"

"Pink in the distance, through the trees. I thought to myself, could we really be this close to the pink house? But, hey, stranger things. Of course the pink disappeared when I began walking in that direction." Her laugh held an embarrassed edge.

"The house is here somewhere." Charlie spoke confidently. "You'll find it again. Or Maisie will find you. I just don't understand why, if you saw it—or thought you did—you didn't wake me to go with you."

"I would have. I just didn't want to wake you if it was simply some crazy reflection."

Something in her voice had him tipping her chin back so their eyes met. "Do you think it was a crazy reflection?"

"I don't know what to think." She blew out a breath. "The house is here, then it's not."

She sounded so miserable that Charlie's heart swelled in sympathy. With a tenderness that surprised them both, he planted a kiss on her forehead. "The pink house is real, Hannah. One day, when the time is right, you'll find it again."

She heaved a sigh. "But not tonight."

"Probably not." He gave her a squeeze, then dropped his arms. "Ready to head back to camp?"

Her blue eyes, so dark in the dim light, searched his. "Thank you for coming to my rescue."

In an attempt to lighten the mood, he shot her a wink. "Anytime a fisher-cat has your back up against a tree, I'm your man."

"I'm going to hold you to that promise." Brushing his mouth with hers, Hannah turned back toward camp.

~

Hannah kept busy over the weekend. She tried not to think of the fact that she'd kissed Charlie Rogan. Well, technically, he'd kissed her first. But his kiss had landed on her forehead, so it barely counted. She'd gone for the mouth.

While the contact had been brief, the feel of her lips on his had unsettled her. She hadn't kissed anyone but Brian for what felt like forever. What was she doing kissing Charlie anyway? And why was she having these feelings for Charlie?

When they'd lowered Brian's casket into the ground, Hannah had vowed that she'd never love anyone else. Now, as the pain of Brian's passing had begun to ease, she realized she had to continue living.

No amount of grieving would bring Brian back. She understood that. Her friendship with Charlie didn't trouble her. It was the desire for him she'd started to experience and a caring that went beyond friendship.

Was this the right time to jump into a relationship? Or was it too soon? Brian's illness and death and all that had followed had changed her in ways she was just now exploring.

Besides, she didn't even know if Charlie's feelings for her went beyond friendship.

Hannah expected—hoped—he might stop by in the days following their camping trip, but she didn't see him, not even out in the yard. On Tuesday, his mother mentioned he was in Baltimore on a business trip.

It was a relief to know he hadn't been avoiding her, that there was a reason for his absence. She could go about her own business without thinking of him. At least for a few days.

When she'd moved back to GraceTown, after what felt like a lifetime of schedules, Hannah had been determined to enjoy the summer and simply take each day as it came.

Yet, every day, even without setting the alarm on her phone, she woke at seven. By seven thirty, the coffee was ready, and she was streaming a yoga workout.

By eight thirty, she was usually on her third cup of coffee, the breakfast dishes were in the dishwasher, and she was ready to work on the house.

Though she'd told herself to forget about Charlie, he was constantly on her mind.

Lisa had mentioned Charlie should be back by Friday, but that day came, and Hannah noticed his truck still wasn't in the driveway. Not that she'd been counting down the days or anything. Like she'd told Mackenna, she and Charlie were neighbors and friends, nothing more.

It was the *nothing more* that didn't ring true. While she certainly didn't want to date him, she enjoyed spending time with him. Enjoyed it a lot.

When Saturday evening rolled around, and his truck still hadn't made an appearance, she decided the neighborly thing to do would be to stop next door and make sure all was well with Lisa.

If, by some chance, she'd missed Charlie pulling his truck into the garage, well, it would be good to see him.

Standing on the Rogans' porch, Hannah noticed the inside of the house was quiet and dark. She gave the door a couple of hard raps. When she got no response, she tried the bell. She knew it worked, because she could hear it ringing.

Hannah waited an extra-long time because, depending on the day, Lisa might be moving slowly. She knocked one more time for good measure and called out, "Lisa, it's Hannah."

She paused and listened intently, but heard no response.

Hannah headed down the steps to the sidewalk, then abruptly came to a stop. What if Lisa had fallen and even now was lying on the floor, unable to get up? What if...

"Her friend picked her up," Geraldine called from across the street. "They're going to the symphony tonight."

Instead of shouting back, Hannah crossed the street, coming to a stop on the sidewalk in front of Beverly and Geraldine's home. "Thanks for letting me know. I told Charlie that if his mom ever needed anything while he was out of town, I'd be available. I wanted to make sure everything was okay."

"Come join us." Geraldine gestured to a wicker rocker that was identical to the one she sat in.

"Us?" Hannah asked.

"Beverly is inside getting sun tea and cookies. When we saw you come out of your house, I told her to bring an extra glass."

"That was nice of you." Hannah climbed the steps to the porch, but hesitated when she reached the rocker. "I don't want to take her seat."

"Beverly likes the swing." Geraldine gestured with one hand to the white lacquered swing swaying gently in the breeze. "That's her favorite spot. I may even join her there once she—"

"Yoo-hoo, could someone open the door for me, please?"

"I'll get it." Hannah motioned Geraldine down and hurried to the screen door.

Beaming, Beverly stepped out onto the porch with a pitcher of tea, three glasses of ice and a plate of what Hannah recognized as Berger cookies.

Her mouth began to water as she thought of the cookies' cakelike bottom topped with a thick fudge spread.

"I haven't had a Berger in years." Hannah's gaze returned to the pretty plate. The sweet treat, originating at a Baltimore bakery back in 1835, was considered by many to be the state cookie of Maryland.

"Then this is your lucky day." Beverly smiled. "Because of blood-sugar issues, one is my limit, so there's plenty here for you and Geraldine."

"Let me set this down for you." Hannah lifted the heavy tray from the older woman's hands and placed it on a white wicker table that matched the porch chairs.

Beverly smiled. "Thank you, hon."

"Did Geraldine tell you that Lisa went to the symphony with her friend?" Beverly bent over the tray, fussing with the contents.

"She did. I was worried—"

"And that Charlie is out on a date?"

"No, no, she didn't mention that." Hannah gratefully took the glass of tea that Geraldine handed her and dropped down into the rocker. "A date? Anyone I know?"

Beverly, who'd made a beeline for the swing after grabbing a cookie on the way, paused. "Ashleigh Christopher. She's a history teacher at one of the high schools. I believe they've gone out before."

Beverly looked to Geraldine and got a confirmatory nod.

"That's nice." Even as her heart twisted, Hannah told herself it didn't matter to her who Charlie dated. "We're just friends."

She started, not having meant to say the reassurance out loud.

When the two women shifted their gazes to her, Hannah smiled weakly.

"Charlie and I," she clarified, though who else could she have been talking about? "We're just friends."

Geraldine and Beverly exchanged glances.

"That's nice," Beverly said when the silence stretched. "I mean, it's nice when neighbors can also be friends. I view most everyone who lives on this block as my friend. Don't you, Geraldine?"

"Most everyone," Geraldine agreed.

"You've been doing some work on your living room, I see," Beverly said.

The woman had given her an out, and Hannah took the change in subject like a running back catching a ball with a clear field ahead.

Hannah might have gone overboard, giving the two women a step-by-step of the progress on the floors and walls. By the time she had them caught up, all thoughts of Charlie were forgotten.

When Hannah finally headed back across the street, she couldn't help but wonder if he'd ever taken the schoolteacher swimming in Devil's Bathtub. Or gone camping in the woods with her.

## CHAPTER FIFTEEN

Hannah spent the next few days sanding and painting. The only time she took a break was to step out on her porch to watch the Independence Day fireworks put on by the city.

She'd hoped she and Mackenna could watch them together, but Mackenna had already made plans with Jace. Next year would be different, Hannah vowed. She'd host a party and invite all her new friends. By then, she'd have a boatload of friends to invite, as well as all her neighbors.

Charlie could bring his girlfriend.

Ignoring the pang that thought evoked, Hannah focused on the house. Despite her phone blaring her favorite tunes, sanding and painting was boring and tedious. She found herself doubting her decision to repaint everything. Perhaps it wouldn't be so bad to leave at least one of the rooms white.

Then she reminded herself that she had the time. Once the living room was painted—and the new furniture arrived—she'd be glad she'd put in the effort.

Taking a lesson learned, Hannah worked on the house, but also took time to play. She read, exercised and contacted a couple of old friends.

Today, she was meeting a friend from high school at the YMCA.

Hannah strode into the modern building, hoping Lydia looked enough like her online pics that she would recognize her. Unlike Hannah and Mackenna, Hannah and Lydia hadn't stayed in touch over the years.

At the desk, Hannah received a warm welcome when she let the receptionist know she was considering joining. With a guest pass in hand, Hannah stepped into the busy atmosphere of the GraceTown Y.

Lydia had suggested they meet by the ellipticals, so Hannah made her way to the fitness area. A long row of machines was set up before windows that looked out over the expansive parking lot.

Hannah scanned the machines, searching for a blond woman about her age.

There were a number of men, some older women, but—

A hand on her shoulder had Hannah whirling.

"Hannah? Hannah Beahr?" Familiar blue eyes in a slightly rounder face than she remembered gazed back at her.

"Lydia." Hannah gave her old friend a hug. "It's Danbury now. I was searching the machines for you."

"My littlest put up a fuss about staying in the nursery. Once I got him settled, I had to drop the other two off at Kids Zone." Lydia smiled. "It's good to see you. I can't believe it's been so long. Do you mind if we work out while we talk?"

"Not at all." Hannah positioned herself on a machine next to Lydia, adjusted the settings, then returned her attention to her friend. The eyes and the wide mouth that appeared curved in a perpetual smile were the same. "You're a brunette now."

Lydia lifted a hand to her straight short bob. "I've embraced all things natural."

"It looks good." Different, Hannah thought, but the warm brown suited her friend's skin tone.

Lydia narrowed her eyes, studying her. "You're still blond."

"My dad said my mother's hair never darkened as she got older. It stayed blond, too." Hannah shifted under her friend's assessing gaze.

"I was sorry to hear about Brian." Lydia offered a sympathetic smile. "I didn't know him in high school. I mean, neither of us did, but he seemed like a good guy."

"He was the best." Hannah had known the subject of Brian would come up, but she was determined not to spend this time with Lydia talking about grief and loss.

While Hannah wasn't averse to updating Lydia on her life prior to moving back to GraceTown, she really wanted to get reacquainted with Lydia, to see if the friendship they'd shared all those years ago could be resurrected. "Tell me what you've been doing since high school."

That's all it took. As they worked out, Lydia updated Hannah on the past ten years of her life.

"I can't believe you're a surgical tech." Hannah's breath came in short puffs as the incline adjusted to nine. "You refused to do a frog dissection in biology."

"That was on principle." Lydia's chin inched up. "Not because I was squeamish."

"Do you like your job?"

"I do." Lydia slowed her movements. "The surgery center is totally fine with me working part-time. Twenty hours a week is all I can handle with three kids under six. Tim is a big help, but I don't want my kids in daycare more than they're with me."

"Until we connected on social media, I didn't realize you had three." That showed just how out of touch they'd been.

"The twins are five. Dylan just turned three." Something that looked a whole lot like pity filled Lydia's eyes. "You and Brian weren't blessed."

Hannah pressed her lips together and reined in her irritation.

"We were waiting to start a family until our careers were firmly on track."

"You were married a long time."

"The month after college graduation."

Lydia's gaze turned speculative. "I can't imagine being married to someone all those years and not wanting to start a family."

What did she say to that? Did she tell Lydia that many, if not most, of the couple friends she and Brian socialized with in Greensboro had had similar plans? And that some of them hadn't been sure they wanted kids at all, and that was okay, too?

Directing the conversation back to Lydia seemed the best course of action. "How long have you and Tim been married?"

"Eight years."

Hannah smiled. "Tell me about your children."

Just like that, they were off to the races. During the next half hour, Hannah heard about how smart the twins were and about Lydia's efforts to potty train Dylan.

Would another woman with children that age find the subject fascinating? As it was, Hannah found it difficult to come up with appropriate questions. She settled for offering encouraging smiles and nodding while perspiration trickled down her temples.

"Tim has a lot of single friends." Lydia's feet were barely moving now. "We could set you up?"

The abrupt change in topic meant one of two things.

Either Lydia was the master of the quick subject change, or when Lydia had launched into how she used M&M's to reward going poopy in the potty, Hannah had spaced out.

"Thank you, but no. I'm not interested in dating right now." Hannah waved a dismissive hand, softening the comment with a smile.

"Brian's been gone over a year." Surprise flickered across

Lydia's face. "That's long enough to grieve. It's time to get on with your life."

It was a variation of what her stepmother had said to her shortly before she and Hannah's dad had left for Florida. Hannah hadn't appreciated the input from Sandie, and she didn't appreciate the push from Lydia now.

"I am getting on with my life." Hannah considered redirecting the conversation one more time, but didn't think she could bear any more toilet-training talk.

Besides, the workout she'd programmed had ended, and she was ready for this reunion to end. She stepped off the machine.

"Well, this has been…" Hannah searched for the right word. Finding none, she settled for, "Nice."

Lydia scrambled off her elliptical.

Reaching over, Hannah put a hand on her arm. "Good luck with the potty training."

"He'll get it one of these days." Lydia kept her voice offhand. "We'll have to do this again sometime."

The fact that Lydia kept plans for any future meetings equally vague told Hannah that she'd also decided that whatever connection they'd shared all those years ago no longer existed.

Like the friends Hannah had left back at Mingus—the women with whom she'd eaten lunch and socialized—they were no longer tied together by something in common, so the connection had dissolved.

Bidding good-bye to Lydia, Hannah slung her bag over her shoulder. She'd taken a risk by contacting Lydia. While it hadn't worked out as she'd hoped, it hadn't been painful.

She thought of her conversation with Maisie, about how people change over time and how that was okay. If future encounters with high school friends were like today's, well, she'd figure out a way to find new friends. Ones who matched the woman she was now, rather than the girl she'd once been. Ones with whom she shared common interests, rather than simply a shared history.

Thankfully, she had Mackenna and Emma.

When Hannah arrived home, her heart gave an excited leap at the sight of Charlie's truck in his driveway. She briefly considered going over to say hello, but squelched the impulse.

Just because she found herself at loose ends didn't give her the right to impose herself on others.

There was still a lot of work to do on the house, but when Hannah stepped inside, instead of changing out of her workout gear, she poured herself a large glass of lemonade and took it, along with Brian's letter, to the porch.

*Fishing on Pigeon Creek at dawn.*

Hannah had never been fishing. She didn't even know how one went about fishing. Were worms always part of the experience? She grimaced at the thought of putting a barb through a living creature.

"What's that look for?"

She jerked her head up, and there he was, looking appealing in worn jeans and a T-shirt.

Hannah lowered the letter. "Hey, you. Where've you been keeping yourself?"

If it wouldn't have been even more lame, Hannah would have groaned aloud. She'd made it sound as if she'd missed him.

"Lots to do lately," was all he said.

She stopped herself—thank goodness she still possessed some restraint—from asking about his schoolteacher girlfriend.

"Me, too." She rested her back against the swing. "I met up with Lydia Poggemeyer at the Y today."

Obviously taking the comment as an invitation to stay, Charlie sat in one of the chairs. "Should that name mean something to me?"

"Probably not. We were friends in high school."

"How was it?" At her blank look, he rolled one hand. "Going down the 'remember when' route."

"Actually, I spent most of the time listening to her efforts to potty train her three-year-old."

Charlie chuckled. "Sounds like fun."

"Not so much." Hannah was tempted to say more, but stopped herself. "It was nice to catch up, but I think it was obvious to both of us that we're at different points in our lives."

"I hear you." Charlie nodded. "There were guys I played ball with in high school. Back then, we were all really tight. Now, unless we're talking football, we really don't have much to say to each other."

"She wanted to set me up with some friends of Tim's. That's her husband," Hannah blurted.

Charlie inclined his head, the look in his brown eyes giving nothing away. "Are you going to let her?"

Hannah made a dismissive sound. "Do you know what she said when I told her I wasn't interested?" She continued, not waiting for Charlie to respond. "She said it had been a year. Like there's some timetable I'm supposed to follow."

"That isn't why you told her you weren't interested."

"What other reason could there be?"

"Lots of them." Charlie lifted a hand and began counting off on his fingers. "For starters, you don't like being pushed. I'm guessing by her mentioning it had been a year, she came across as pushy. Am I right?"

Hannah expelled a breath. "Yes. What else?"

He smiled slightly. "You don't know her husband, or you do know him and don't like him. Either way, you don't trust his judgment."

"I don't like him. During our freshman year, I heard him making pig noises when Barbi Dunlop walked by." Hannah's fingers tightened around her glass of lemonade. Simply recalling the incident had anger rising all over again. "I confronted him, asked what his father—his dad was a minister—would think of him treating a person with such disrespect."

"How did he respond?"

"He told me Barbi wasn't a person, she was a pig." Hannah pressed her lips together. "His friends laughed. I reported the incident to the principal. On my way home, I stopped by his father's church and told his dad what I'd observed."

"You had balls." Admiration shown in Charlie's dark eyes. "What happened?"

"I don't know. I never witnessed that behavior from him again. But our paths didn't often cross, so..." She lifted her shoulders and let them drop. "I could only hope what I did made a difference."

"I can understand why you wouldn't want to go on a date with one of his friends."

"Not in this lifetime." Hannah wondered how Lydia could have married him. Maybe he'd changed. For Lydia's sake, she hoped so.

"You're reading Brian's letter." Charlie gestured to the paper in her lap.

"I'm considering going fishing."

Charlie leaned back in his seat, not appearing surprised. "When are you planning to go?"

"I have to do some research first." She took a sip of lemonade, then realized she hadn't offered him any. "Can I get you something to drink?"

"I'm fine." He cocked his head. "What kind of research?"

"Everything." She gave an embarrassed laugh. "I've never been fishing. I thought I'd look up what kind of fish are in Pigeon Creek and which ones bite at dawn. Then I need to research bait alternatives to worms. I'm not about to put a worm on a hook. I don't care if fish like worms best. Worms are off the table."

"Not a worm fan." He grinned. "I get it."

"I need to pick up a fishing pole or rod—I don't really know the difference." Hannah expelled a breath. "All this work hardly seems worth it for one time. Yet, I want to do it."

"I can help you. If you want my help, that is." Charlie held up both hands, palms out.

"I'll take any help you can give me."

"Brian and I hooked a lot of blue catfish in Pigeon Creek. We used a beer meal catfish bait. The fish love it, and no worms are killed in the making."

Hannah smiled. "Now I guess I only need to find a pole. Or rod."

"I've got a couple of catfish rods."

"You don't mind bringing an extra with you for me?"

Charlie sat up a little straighter. "You want me to come with you?"

Hannah realized she'd just assumed he meant to come along. "I know you're busy. I shouldn't have presumed—"

"I want to come." The tension in his shoulders eased, and he visibly relaxed. "And yes, I have rods for both of us. You just need to tell me when you want to go."

"I'd love to go tomorrow. If that doesn't work for you—"

His hand closed around hers, stilling her nervous chatter.

She should pull away, casually slip her fingers from the warmth of his hand, but she couldn't bring herself to do it.

He was the one to finally break the connection by giving her hand a squeeze, then sitting back. "Tomorrow works. Can you be ready at five thirty?"

Hannah nodded. "Is there anything special I should wear?"

"I'll bring a couple of lawn chairs. Wear something old so if you get dirty, it won't matter. Oh, and if you have a pair of rubber boots, bring those."

"I can do that."

Pushing back his chair, he rose. "I'll see you bright and early."

"I'm looking forward to it."

Was it only wishful hearing, or did he say, "Me, too" as he strode off the porch in the direction of his house?

# CHAPTER SIXTEEN

"You are not going fishing in the morning." Emma's peal of laughter at the other end of the phone line grated.

After chatting about Calista's pregnancy, Emma had turned her attention to Hannah. Almost immediately, Hannah regretted mentioning her plans for tomorrow.

"I told you about Brian's letter, Em." Hannah did her best to not let her annoyance show in her voice. "Fishing is something he got pleasure out of, something he wished he'd shared with me."

"But fishing. Worms. Yuck."

"Charlie promised no worms would die."

"You're going with Charlie?"

Something in Emma's voice put Hannah on alert. "I told you that."

"No," Emma clarified. "You said you were going fishing at dawn. You didn't say one word about Charlie coming with you."

"Oversight." Hannah kept her tone matter-of-fact. "He's got the knowledge, the poles and the bait. It makes sense for us to go together."

"You've been spending a lot of time with him."

"Not that much." Hannah hated the defensive edge to her

voice and fought to smooth it. "Until yesterday, it had been nearly a week since we even talked."

"A week, eh? Sounds like you're keeping count."

Hannah knew her friend was teasing, but she also realized she *had* been keeping count. Why was that?

"I don't have many friends here yet, Em." Hannah leaned her head back against the sofa. "Mackenna is busy with work and her other activities. I'm doing my best to reach out. I tried with Lydia. That was a bust."

"It'll take time." Emma's voice softened.

"I know that." Hannah hesitated, then plunged ahead. "I enjoy talking with Charlie. We have fun together."

"Do you like him?"

"Of course I like him."

"No, I mean, do you like him like a guy you want to date?"

Hannah's knee-jerk was to say no, to tell Emma what she'd told Lydia, that it was too soon for her to think about dating anyone. But she admitted to herself that if she were to date anyone, if she *were* interested in dating anyone, it would be Charlie.

"He's a good guy," Hannah conceded. "I'm not sure I'm ready to date, but if I were, yes, I'd consider him."

Emma said nothing for several long seconds. "Don't take this the wrong way, and God knows you know this better than I do, but life doesn't come with guarantees. Don't wait too long."

"I don't know if dating me would be fair to Charlie."

"Why wouldn't it?"

"I loved Brian. Can you really love more than one man? I mean, really love them?" Hannah thought of her father. "My dad married Sandie. He says he loves her. Does he love Sandie as much as he loved my mom? I don't know. I'd say no, but maybe that's just what I want to believe."

"Don't worry so much. Even when we plan, there're curve balls. Take it a day at a time. If you're moving forward, you're making progress." Emma paused. "Speaking of moving forward, are you still planning to apply for that position at Collister for this fall?"

Hannah hesitated for only a second. "Actually, I've always loved baking, so I'm considering giving that a try."

Silence filled the air for several heartbeats.

"I know you enjoy baking, but you never said anything about wanting to pursue it as a career."

Though Emma tried hard to hide it, Hannah heard both hurt and concern in her friend's voice.

Hannah waved an airy hand. "It's one of many options I'm considering."

"You'll make the right decision."

"I will." Hannah only wished she knew the right way to go.

With so many thoughts swirling in her head, Hannah wondered if she'd sleep, but she dropped off the second her head hit the pillow.

The alarm on her phone had her jerking straight up in bed, her heart pounding. She'd been dreaming. Charlie had been kissing her. And she'd been kissing him back.

Even now, her blood still flowed hot and fast.

Taking several deep breaths, she fought for composure. Today was about fishing. About Brian. Not about kissing Charlie.

Thankfully, she'd laid out her clothes the night before. Not that it took much to pull on a pair of paint-splattered jeans, a T-shirt and an oversized sweatshirt.

It could be cool in the mornings, so she wanted to make sure she was warm enough, but she wasn't certain how long they'd be out there, or how hot it would get once the sun came out.

Either way, she was prepared.

Hannah slid her feet into slip-on sneakers, grabbed her boots and headed out the front door with five minutes to spare.

Charlie waited by his truck. He wore jeans and a light jacket over a T-shirt. As she approached, his gaze traveled all the way from her feet to her head, leaving a trail of heat in its wake.

"Do I meet with your approval?" she asked in a flippant tone.

He nodded approvingly at her layers. "I have hats in the truck in case the sun gets hot, but they can stay where they are for now. You look good."

Hannah couldn't help the flush of pleasure. "So do you."

He grinned and opened the passenger door. "Now that we've got that settled, let's go."

She'd spent time along Pigeon Creek as a girl. The church youth group she'd attended had had several gatherings along the creek bank.

The area where Charlie took her was farther down and more isolated. They had to pick their way through some brush before stepping into an opening.

Charlie slanted a glance in her direction. "This is the spot where Brian and I always came to fish."

Hannah stared at the place on the bank. For a second, she saw Brian sitting there, flashing that megawatt smile that always turned her knees to mush.

Her heart swelled.

Tears filled her eyes.

She started at Charlie's hand on her shoulder. "This is a good spot filled with happy memories," he said softly.

"We'll make more today." Blinking back the moisture, Hannah set up the chairs while he set out the tackle box and rods.

"We'll bait the hook with my special mixture." Charlie showed her how it was done on one hook, then gestured for her to do the same on the other.

Hannah sensed if she demurred and asked him to bait hers, he'd oblige. She reminded herself that she was here to learn.

There was no better time to do that than when she had a teacher with her, one who could answer any questions she might have.

"What kind of catfish will we catch?"

"There's predominantly blue around here."

"What's in this stuff?" She carefully put the bait on the circular hook, then gladly took the rag Charlie extended to wipe off her fingers.

He shot her a wink. "You don't want to know."

Charlie spent the next few minutes showing her how to cast her line. "Since we're staying in one place, we need to cast it way out there."

She smiled triumphantly when hers finally was where it needed to be. "Now what do we do?"

"We sit and we wait."

"How long will that take?" Hannah studied the water, felt for the slightest movement in her pole.

"Hard to say. Usually within fifteen to twenty minutes. It could be longer."

"Longer?" Hannah pulled her brows together. "What do we do while we're waiting?"

He reached into a zippered bag and pulled out two insulated coffee tumblers. "We enjoy our morning coffee."

Hannah took the mug and flipped open the top, inhaling the rich Colombian flavor. "Thank you."

He'd already taken his first sip. "You're welcome."

"But seriously, what do we do?"

"We sit here. Relax."

"Just sit here?"

"Yep." He smiled. "Nothing says we can't talk while we wait. Yelling is off the table, though, because it'd scare the fish."

Hannah took another long sip of coffee and tried to imagine her type-A, always-on-the-go husband simply sitting here when there were a thousand and one other things he could be doing.

"I can see that mind of yours working overtime." Charlie gazed at her over the top of his mug. "What's the conclusion?"

Unlike with some people, Hannah didn't feel the need to censor her words or thoughts with Charlie.

"I didn't know Brian other than by sight in high school. He struck me as ambitious even back then." Hannah wrapped her fingers around the mug. "That's how he was during our years together. It was difficult to get him to relax or take any downtime."

"What about you?"

"Me?" Her voice rose.

"You dove into your home improvements without pausing to catch a breath after you moved back," he observed. "It seems you've always got some kind of list going."

"I also took time this week to sit on my porch and relax."

Cocking his head, he only studied her.

"What?"

"You didn't answer my question." His tone gentled. "I can see you're making an effort to have a balanced life. What I asked, though, is how were you back in Greensboro?"

Hannah chewed on her bottom lip. Thinking about the past had her insides churning. No matter how she spun it, there were so many things she'd have done differently, better.

But she'd learned this last year that life moved on with few do-overs and to not take for granted the time she was given.

"For a long time, I was as driven as Brian. I threw myself into my job with the goal of moving up, of becoming an employee they couldn't do without." She gave a little laugh. "We see how that worked out."

Charlie relaxed further into the lawn chair. "It sounds as if what you wanted changed even before they gave you the heave-ho."

As he took a long sip of coffee, his gaze remained on her face.

If she'd seen judgment there, she wouldn't have responded.

"A year or so before Brian got sick, I sensed my passion for the job waning." She sipped her coffee, and the caffeine gave her system the jolt it needed. "My duties had begun to seem pointless. I wanted something…different."

"What did Brian have to say when you mentioned how you were feeling?"

"I never said anything to him."

"Why not?" Surprise skittered across Charlie's face. "I'm sure he'd have been supportive of you making a change."

Hannah couldn't hide her doubt. "I'm not so sure. Brian never deviated from his plans."

"You're not giving him enough credit. He was supportive of me dropping out of school when no one else was."

"What about your mom?"

Charlie shook his head. "Not at first. She felt guilty, as if she was the one pulling me away from completing my education. The truth was, I'd gotten out of my two years what I needed to pursue my dreams."

Hannah recalled how surprised she'd been when her husband had defended Charlie for leaving college. Brian had insisted that Charlie was brilliant and knew what he was doing. "Brian always said leaving MIT was the right choice for you."

"His acceptance, his openness to considering that others might have dreams that didn't mirror his own, was one of the things I admired most about him."

Hannah heard the affection in his voice. "You miss him."

"Darn right I do." Charlie gazed out over the water and cleared his throat. "He was an amazing man and friend."

"I miss him, too."

Charlie's hand reached over and covered hers. He didn't say anything more. His hand simply remained on hers as they sat on the bank of the creek, the rising sun casting a golden glow over the water.

"His death has made me realize tomorrow isn't guaranteed. I

don't want to spend time at a job that doesn't fulfill me." Hannah thought of how Mackenna and Emma had reacted when she told them she was considering a career in baking.

"Makes sense to me." Charlie sipped his coffee, his gaze watchful. "If you didn't love what you were doing, why go back into that field?"

"Making a go of the baking thing is a long shot."

"Long shots come in every day." He offered an encouraging smile. "Why not at least try? Who cares if you fail? You can always try something else. You can always change your mind."

"It feels like everyone I know believes the smart thing for me to do is to get the best position possible with the best pay and benefits."

"They aren't you." Charlie took another long drink of coffee. "I'm glad you're taking your time and not rushing a decision."

Hannah just nodded.

"Shifting directions can be challenging, especially when the road you're traveling is filled with unexpected surprises."

"Like the letter I got from the woman in the woods."

"That was definitely a surprise."

Before Hannah could reply, her pole jerked, and the force pulled the rod from her hand.

# CHAPTER SEVENTEEN

The rod was barely free of Hannah's hand when Charlie clamped his fingers around it.

"Take it," he ordered, shoving the rod back at her.

She obeyed, but gazed wide-eyed at him, a look of panic on her face. "What do I do?"

"First, don't let go." He kept his tone calm, almost matter-of-fact. "We don't know how good he's hooked, so you don't want to jerk and maybe lose him."

"He's strong." Hannah's fingers tightened around the rod.

Charlie flashed a smile. "Now you're going to slowly reel him in."

"I don't know how to do that." She stood now, both hands wrapped around the rod.

"That's what I'm here for." Pushing to his feet, he got behind her and put his arms around her.

For a second, she shuddered.

"No reason to be scared. You've got this." Despite the feel of her soft body in his arms doing a number on his concentration, Charlie did his best to block out everything except the task at hand. He wasn't about to have her first fishing expedition end in disaster.

His hands remained over hers as he assessed the pull and the pressure in the line. "It's time to reel him in."

She turned her head ever so slightly, her cheek brushing against his stubble as she lifted questioning eyes to his.

"Like this." He showed her how to slowly reel in the fish. "Don't let go of the pole while you do it."

She chuckled. "Letting go would be counterproductive."

"I can't wait to see what you hooked."

"That makes two of us." She set her jaw, and the rod bowed as she continued to draw the fish closer to shore.

Charlie was beginning to think the fish would never make an appearance when it broke free of the surface. "That's okay. Keep him there. Let him swim and splash around for a bit."

With fishing gloves on, he moved forward, ignoring the sucking sound of mud under his boots.

"It's huge." Hannah gazed in awe at the fish. "And so pretty."

A chuckle escaped his lips. Charlie didn't know many people who'd call a catfish of any variety pretty. Reaching down, he grasped the catfish behind its three front spines.

Hannah craned her neck to see better. "What are you doing?"

"It's important to hold it behind the spines located on the edges of its dorsal and pectoral fins," Charlie answered as he made his way to shore with the wiggling fish. "When catfish feel threatened, they lock out their spines. If those spines happened to puncture your hand or your arm, it hurts like hell."

"Don't let him hurt you."

"Under control." He smiled, keeping his tone reassuring as he stepped onto dry land.

"How big is he?" Hannah asked, her eyes wide and very blue.

After studying the fish more closely, Charlie gave his best guess. "I'd say ten pounds."

"How big do they get?"

"The last I knew, the state record for blue was eighty-four pounds."

Some of the light left her eyes. "Not so big, then."

"A nice size for your first. Keep or toss?" he asked.

A funny look crossed her face. "What?"

"The fish." He gestured with his head toward the fish. "If you want to keep him, we'll put him in that bucket, then clean him and cook him later. Or we can toss him back to be caught another day. You reeled him in, so it's your call."

Hannah chewed on her bottom lip and considered. This only confirmed what Charlie had already discovered about her. She wasn't a woman who made snap decisions. Her moves were carefully thought out.

After several seconds, she slanted a glance at him. "I'd like a picture of the three of us, then I want to set him free."

"Just so you're aware, catching and releasing catfish is discouraged." When he saw Hannah's brow furrow, Charlie spoke quickly. "But since we're putting him back in the same body of water where we got him, it's okay."

Relief washed across her face, followed quickly by concern. "How will you get the hook out?"

"Team effort." Charlie gestured with his head. "There're pliers and a line cutter in the pack beside my chair. Bring them over."

Hannah quickly complied, carrying one in each hand to him. "Which do you want first?"

"First, I want you to cut the line. About six inches from the fish."

With rock-steady hands, Hannah snipped.

"Good." Charlie nodded approval and held out his hand. "Now, the pliers."

Flipping around the pliers so Charlie could grasp the handle, she held them out to him, then leaned forward. "What are you going to do?"

"I'm going to grab hold of the eye of the hook." His attention remained on the fish as he illustrated the maneuver, then said, "I'm rolling the hook's eye toward the hook's point. Then I'll twist the hook's point and," he smiled, "pull it out of the catfish's lip."

"Yay." Hannah beamed at him. "Now you can toss it back."

"Sometimes you have to burp them. But he shows no signs of distension. You brought him up slowly, and allowing him to splash around on the surface helped. As did me holding him with the belly down while taking out the hook." Charlie studied the fish. "I see no evidence that his swim bladder is distended, so he should be good to go."

"Let me get my camera first." Hannah hurried to his side and held out her phone, capturing the two of them and the fish.

With the catfish firmly in hand, Charlie strode back into the muck, then slipped the fish back into the water.

He smiled as it swam away.

When he returned to shore, she shoved her camera into his hands. "Could you take a few pictures of me with my fishing reel?"

"Happy to." Charlie stepped back. He took a couple of shots and was adjusting the camera to take more when she called out, "Maybe if I shift this way, the sun won't—"

Hannah took a couple steps back, then shrieked as her feet sank into a hole. Her arms windmilled as she and the fishing rod hit the water at the same time.

Shoving the camera into his jacket, he locked his hands around her wrists and pulled her from the murky water. She stumbled to the shore, losing one canvas shoe in the process.

"That was quite a splash."

Hannah surprised him when she laughed, wiping a dripping strand of hair from her face and leaving a streak of dirt on her forehead. "I always say when you go, you might as well go big."

She glanced down at her soaked and muddy clothes. "It appears this fishing expedition has come to a splashing end."

"I didn't notice the hole. I should have—"

"Not your fault." Hannah reached out as if to touch his arm, but pulled back at the last minute. "I didn't see it either. You know, I've never fallen into a creek before. It's a once-in-a-life-time experience."

"You're being an awfully good sport."

She smiled and inched farther from the edge of the stream. "I've had fun today. Is fishing always this exciting?"

"Not always." Charlie smiled back. "Though it usually is relaxing."

"You know what I'd like to do now?"

"What?" Charlie had the feeling he knew. He tried to hide his disappointment at having their outing cut short.

"I'd like to go home, shower and change clothes."

Charlie nodded. Just as he'd thought.

"Then I'd like to take you out for breakfast at that new place on Lillibridge Road. My treat."

He couldn't stop his smile.

"Unless you're busy," she added, obviously mistaking his silence.

He wasn't sure what got into him. Truly, when he looked back, Charlie wondered just what he'd been thinking when he slung an arm around her shoulders and kissed her lightly on the mouth. "Never too busy for you."

Conscious of Charlie waiting for her in the living room, Hannah kept the shower short. She did wash her hair, a necessity since the blond stands held a fishy smell in addition to streaks of mud. That smell carried through to her body and her clothes that now lay in a tangled mess on the bathroom floor.

Once all the mud and muck had swirled down the drain,

Hannah dressed quickly, pulling on a pair of white shorts with a bright blue tee.

Since one of her canvas shoes remained stuck in the muck of Pigeon Creek, she donned a pair of strappy sandals.

"I'm ready," she called out.

Charlie glanced up from his phone. "Wow. Not only do you look amazing, you cleaned up in record time."

"That's because I'm starving."

Charlie untangled his tall body from the sofa and rose, all six feet one of handsome male. "Falling into a creek will do that to you."

She narrowed her gaze. "You're wearing a different shirt."

"Am I?" A smile tugged at the corners of his lips even as his expression remained innocent.

Hannah was positive, well, nearly positive that this was a different shirt. It was his almost smile that had her pressing forward. "Yes, you are."

She stepped close, though why she wasn't sure. It certainly wasn't necessary for the conversation. Hannah fingered the hem of the faded MIT T-shirt, then sniffed. "Yep. Definitely different."

This time, he blasted a full smile in her direction. "While you were showering, I ran home and took one of my own. Couldn't go out for breakfast smelling fishy with a beautiful woman."

"Looks like we're ready, then."

Instead of crossing the yard to where his truck was parked, when they reached her driveway, Hannah gestured to her hybrid SUV. "Let's take mine."

"I was hoping for a ride in this."

"Do I need to open the door for you?" she asked, recalling his insistence on doing that for her.

"I believe I can manage." He slid into the passenger seat. "How do you like it?"

"I love it." They kept the windows down as they drove downtown, the breeze drying the edges of her hair, still damp from her shower.

"There's a community parking lot behind the food market," Charlie told her. "You're more likely to find a parking spot there than on the street."

He was right about both. "I didn't even know this lot existed."

"The city put in a number of these public lots several years back. I was on one of the committees that studied the issue."

She cut the engine, then shifted in her seat to face him. "I didn't know you were into city planning."

"I was a community representative." He shrugged. "I don't have any education in city planning, if that's what you're asking, but this town is my home. I care about the decisions made by those in command."

"When we lived in Greensboro," Hannah said as she exited the car, then fell into step beside Charlie, "I barely knew who the mayor was, let alone had any interest in where they put their parking lots."

"I'm betting at that point you weren't sure if you were staying." Not waiting for her to answer, he continued. "Once you knew for sure that would be your home, and once you had more time, I bet you'd have paid more attention."

Chowtown sat in the middle of the block. The outdoor seating area of the popular eatery sported several open tables.

Hannah caught the gleam in Charlie's eyes as he took note of the empty tables.

"Are you thinking what I'm thinking?" she asked.

He grinned. "That food might be on the table quicker than we thought possible? I'm hopin'."

It was an accurate prediction. They scored one of the outdoor tables, and the server, Niki, told them they were her first customers, as she'd just started her shift.

Immediately after they ordered, Niki reappeared with cups of steaming coffee as well as two complimentary bite-sized pieces of cinnamon roll.

Hannah gazed at the gooey rolls. "That could ruin my appetite."

"Don't eat one, then. More for me," was Charlie's response as he popped one into his mouth.

"Is it good?" Hannah leaned forward.

Charlie widened his eyes, then a devilish gleam sparked in them. He shook his head as he chewed.

But when he reached for her piece, she snatched it up. "No, you don't, mister. I—"

"Charlie. Hi."

The greeting came from the sidewalk.

When they both turned, the attractive brunette widened her smile to include Hannah. "This is a surprise."

Charlie pushed to his feet, an easy smile on his face. "Ashleigh, it's good to see you."

"You told me you were doubling down on finalizing your latest design."

He lifted his hands, let them drop, that easy smile never wavering. "A man has to eat."

"Of course you do. I'm just—" The brunette stopped. "I'm surprised to see you here."

"Hannah, this is Ashleigh Christopher. Ashleigh teaches history at Westgate."

Ashleigh nodded, her curious gaze now firmly fixed on Hannah.

"Ashleigh, this is Hannah Danbury. Hannah is—"

"I remember you mentioning her. The wife of your best friend."

"Actually, the widow of his best friend." Feeling at a disadvantage with the other two standing, Hannah pulled to her feet. She extended a hand, which Ashleigh shook. "It's nice to meet you."

"Good to meet you." Ashleigh shot another glance in Charlie's direction. "With school out, I have more free time. Give me a call if you want to get together."

Hannah expelled a breath seconds later when Ashleigh strode away. She didn't have time to say anything to Charlie before Niki arrived with their food.

"Well, that was awkward," Hannah said once Niki topped off their coffee and left.

Charlie added a swath of grape jelly to his toast, looked up. "What was awkward?"

"Ashleigh." Hannah shifted in her seat. "It was clear, at least to me, that she thinks I'm encroaching on her territory."

His dark eyes met hers. "I'm not anyone's territory."

"I know you don't think that." Hannah waved an airy hand even as her heart twisted. "But you've been dating her and—"

Charlie's hand closing over hers stopped the words and had her heart hammering. "While it's true Ashleigh and I have gone out a couple of times, before the weekend of the Fourth, it had been months."

"Because you've been busy," Hannah began.

His fingers tightened around hers. "I make time for what's important. With Ashleigh, there's no spark. Not like with you."

She inhaled sharply.

"Some people you just feel closer to from the get-go." Releasing her hand, he offered a careless shrug. "All that to say you're not encroaching on anything. Understand?"

Unable to find her voice after his declaration, Hannah simply gave a jerky nod before focusing on her food.

Charlie started talking about his latest project, and while Hannah didn't understand half of what he was saying, his enthusiasm had her relaxing.

Was there anything more compelling than a man—or woman —pursuing their passion? Brian had found his. So had Charlie.

She, well, she'd *identified* a passion. Now, it was time for her to pursue it.

# CHAPTER EIGHTEEN

Hannah spent the next two weeks researching steps she needed to take to start a home baking business. After much thought, she'd decided not to pursue a job at one of the local establishments. She was discovering a retail bakery was a far different animal than the type of business she hoped to run.

It made more sense to use her time researching trademarks and health and safety rules as well as delving into the ins and outs of various social media platforms. And, of course, fine-tuning recipes. With each step forward, she took time to relax and celebrate.

She thought about Maisie often, but despite several forays into the woods, she had yet to spot her or the house again.

Hannah saw Charlie frequently. With him living right next door, it was inevitable. She'd come to look forward to their late-night talks on her porch.

Over a glass of wine, he'd tell her about progress on his latest project, and she'd update him on her day. Sometimes, in addition to a glass of wine, he would get to sample her latest baking masterpiece.

She lifted a hand in acknowledgment when Charlie called out

to her as he strode across the lawn and made short work of the steps.

"What do you have for me this time?" He smiled and pointed to the two slices of cake sitting on the table.

"I've been working on tweaking a recipe for white wedding cake with vanilla frosting." Hannah handed him a glass of wine. "As the Riesling is slightly sweet, it will bring out the flavors in the vanilla cake."

"Happy to be your guinea pig." Charlie lifted the colorful plate that was part of her wedding china.

Hannah watched his mouth close over the big bite of cake, then let out the breath she hadn't realized she'd been holding when his lips curved in a broad smile.

He held up a finger and washed the cake down with a sip of wine before speaking. "Incredible."

"You really like it?"

His gaze met hers. "I love it."

"Good." She lifted her own plate and forked off a bite. As the flavors filled her mouth, she analyzed, then nodded.

"Told you it was incredible." Charlie took another sip of wine. "How's the other research coming?"

This was one of the things she'd discovered about Charlie. Their interactions didn't have to be all about him. He always appeared genuinely interested in her progress.

"I've decided on a name."

He inclined his head.

"Hannah Cakes." During her trademark search, she'd discovered many of the names she'd initially considered were already taken. "No trademark on either the federal or state level. The domain is available, and I can get the username on social media platforms."

"I like it. Another step forward." Charlie lifted his glass and motioned for her to do the same. He clinked his glass against hers. "To Hannah Cakes."

Hannah couldn't stop the surge of pleasure. "This is really going to happen."

"Did you have any doubts?" Charlie relaxed against the back of his chair and took another bite of cake.

"There is more to launching a home-based business than I thought," she admitted, thinking of the upcoming appointment with the attorney to form an LLC and register for an EIN. "Lots of business chinks to work out."

Charlie's gaze turned thoughtful. "You know what I've noticed about you?"

"What?"

"Several things, actually." He took a long drink of wine, then his glass. "This really does go well with the cake."

"Told you." She kept her voice light, even though everything inside seemed filled with a watchful waiting. "You were saying?"

"Your resilience. Despite everything that has happened to you, you keep going. Starting a new business isn't easy, but you're pushing forward and doing what needs to be done."

"Thank you, Charlie." The flush of pleasure she experienced at the compliment had her wanting to hear more. "You mentioned...several things?"

"You're rocking this self-care thing."

Bringing her glass to her lips, she peered at him over the rim, her brows pulling together. "Self-care thing?"

"You work hard, but you're taking time to relax and enjoy all life has to offer."

"Does sitting on the porch with you most nights count as part of all life has to offer?" she teased.

He didn't smile back. "I know there are likely a thousand things on your plate that you could be working on right now."

"Same goes for you, buddy."

Charlie's gaze met hers. "Believe me when I say there is no other place I'd rather be than right here with you."

The night air pulsed as her eyes locked with his for several erratic heartbeats. Hannah would not, simply *could* not, look away.

She moistened her suddenly dry lips with the tip of her tongue and watched his eyes go dark.

Without taking his eyes off her, Charlie set down his plate and leaned forward. "Hannah, I—"

The throaty rumble of a motorcycle stilled whatever he'd been about to say. Her gaze and Charlie's shifted at the same moment to see Sean O'Malley cruise down the quiet street on a Harley.

Hannah cleared her throat. "I didn't know Sean had a motorcycle."

"He got it last year. This is the first I've seen him on it this summer." Charlie started to say more, but Hannah spoke first.

"You don't have a motorcycle, do you?"

He blinked. "No, why do you ask?"

"Just wondering."

As if realizing that the moment they'd shared only seconds earlier had been shattered, Charlie appeared to switch gears. "In high school, Brian and I were crazy about motorcycles. Remember that place out on the highway where you could rent those small bikes?"

"Mike's?"

"That's the one." Charlie grinned at the memory. "I can't tell you the number of times Brian and I would rent a bike and take off with no particular destination in mind."

"That spontaneity must have driven Brian crazy. He was such a planner."

Charlie smiled. "Not so much back then."

"You guys wouldn't have even been eighteen. I can't believe Mike let you rent a motorcycle."

Charlie shrugged. "We were seventeen, so old enough. Mike wasn't particular who he rented to. We had to drive around the parking lot to show him we knew how to handle the bike, then we'd hand over our money and take off."

Hannah brought a hand to her head and shuddered. "You could have been killed."

"You're right about that." Charlie's expression turned rueful. "I guess you could say we were lucky."

"Where did you go?"

"It varied. The Catoctin Mountain Orchard became a favorite destination." Charlie's eyes warmed with memories. "It wasn't that far, and we discovered lots of hot girls live in Thurmont."

Hannah just rolled her eyes.

"Really hot girls," Charlie told her.

"I get the picture. While I'm not a fan of motorcycles, taking a road trip on one does sound like fun." Hannah heard the wistfulness in her voice. "I wish I could have experienced a few of those adventures."

"With Brian?"

Hannah shrugged and smiled, leaving him to draw his own conclusion.

"Brian and I talked about riding to Baltimore to watch the Orioles play." Charlie reached for his wineglass and took a sip. "Never happened."

"Let's do it. You and me." Hannah's voice shook with eagerness. "We'll rent motorcycles and watch a game at Camden Yards."

His eyes widened, then narrowed. "Do you know how to drive a motorcycle?"

"I can learn." Hannah waved a dismissive hand. "If you and Brian could do it at seventeen, I can do it at thirty."

"I like your spirit." Lifting his glass in a mock toast, he took a sip. "We'll make this a celebratory trip."

Hannah inclined her head. "Just what will we be celebrating?"

"How about all the progress you've made toward opening Hannah Cakes?"

"Starting a business feels right," she told him, unable to keep from smiling. "Even if it doesn't work out—"

"Stop that." Charlie reached over and took her hand, his brown eyes firmly focused on her face. "You're not going to fail. You've got mad baking skills and a background in marketing. You've reached out to the local Women in Business group, and there are great resources there. And I hope you know that I'm here if you need me."

"Your support means so much." Hannah kept her tone deliberately light.

"Happy to do whatever I can to aid in your success." His lips quirked upward. "Except bake."

She laughed. "When should we take off on this grand adventure?"

"There's a four o'clock game this Saturday with the Angels." His tone turned offhand. "We could have dinner on the water after."

"If you already had plans to go, I don't want to intrude."

"No plans."

"You just happen to know when the O's play?"

"Does that day and time work for you?"

"It does." She hesitated. "We should probably do a couple motorcycle trial runs before then."

"It'd probably be best if you ride with me this first time."

"Okay. That works, too." Hannah impulsively lifted her glass. After a second, he lifted his. "To new adventures."

When the crystal rang out as the glasses tapped together, Hannah told herself that this trip was simply something new and fun for her to do. And, like Charlie had said, it would make her feel connected to Brian.

But as Hannah gazed into Charlie's dark eyes, she knew that the excitement that shot through her had nothing to do with Brian and everything to do with Charlie.

~

Baking cupcakes for a fundraiser in the town square kept Hannah busy early Saturday morning. When she got in her car to head downtown at nine, she spotted Charlie backing out of his driveway.

She honked and pulled up next to his truck on the street, sliding down her window. "Did you get the bike?"

"Everything is in place. I have our transportation, tickets to the game and a parking space secured."

"I've been looking forward to this all week." She thought of Hugh and chuckled. "Unlike our neighbor, I'm very glad that the rain went north. Again."

Charlie smiled. "Does leaving at one still work for you?"

"I'll be ready. See you then." Lifting a hand in farewell, she sped off down the street.

After spending a couple of hours at the Women in Business booth handing out cupcakes and coupons good for 25% off an initial Hannah Cakes order, Hannah realized Charlie had been right. These women were not only great resources, but also a built-in support system. She could even see a couple of them becoming close friends.

As she drove home, Hannah thought how her life continued to become richer in ways she had never imagined.

Once she got home, she changed into leggings and a cute black shirt she'd picked up this week that boasted thin pinstripes of orange. Orange wasn't really her color, but this *was* an Orioles game.

Besides, as casual as the shirt was, she could dress it up by ditching the Orioles cap. When deciding what to wear, Hannah had kept not only the motorcycle in mind, but also Charlie's comment about grabbing dinner afterward on the water.

Hannah moved to the mirror near the front door and added more color to her lips, then gave herself one last glance.

With her hair pulled back in a jaunty tail and the ball cap on her head, she could easily pass for a college student heading out to watch some baseball.

She felt like one, excited and unsure. When her phone dinged, and she saw it was a text from Charlie asking her to come outside, she was ready.

Ready to forget the heartache of the past for one evening and simply embrace new possibilities.

# CHAPTER NINETEEN

As Hannah stepped from her porch, Beverly paused in her watering across the street to lift a hand and wave.

Waving back, Hannah came to an abrupt halt when she spotted Charlie. He wasn't on a motorcycle, but rather, stood in her driveway next to a sleek vintage Jaguar convertible.

She crossed quickly to him, conscious of Beverly's gaze following her as she stopped beside the car. She pointed. "This doesn't look like a motorcycle to me."

Dressed in jeans and an Orioles jersey, Charlie grinned. "You've got sharp eyes. I had a feeling you'd notice."

She ran her fingers appreciatively over the glossy red paint. "This isn't what you and Brian had planned."

"If we'd had the money and the ability to rent such a car, we'd have done it in a heartbeat." Reaching down, he opened her door. "Milady, your chariot awaits."

"You're such a dork." She swatted him with the back of her hand before settling into the plush leather seat. "I like your style."

Hannah discovered she also liked riding in the car with Charlie. Though she had to admit she wouldn't have minded making the hour drive with her front pressed to his back and her arms wrapped around him.

She couldn't say what they talked about on their way to Baltimore, only that conversation came easily. Of course, it always did when she was with him.

Once they reached the Charm City, Charlie pulled the Jag into a multilevel parking garage. Steering the car into its assigned spot, he smiled in satisfaction at the wall on one side and the amount of room between the Jag and the vehicle on the passenger side. "This was the best parking I could reserve on such late notice. It's about a mile walk to Camden Yards. You cool with that?"

"The walk is an added plus." Hannah flashed a smile. "It'll give me an opportunity to fully experience the game-day atmosphere."

The smile Charlie offered her had everything in her going warm. He reached behind her seat and pulled out a ball cap, settling it on his head. "When in Baltimore…"

Hannah chuckled, and when he rounded the back of the car to open her door for her, she took his arm as if it were the most natural thing in the world.

As soon as they stepped out of the parking garage onto the sidewalk, they found themselves surrounded by Orioles fans.

The excited chatter and laughter buoyed Hannah's mood to a fever pitch. She found herself squeezing Charlie's arm more tightly. "I can't believe we're here."

He glanced down at her. "I'm glad we're doing this."

"Me, too."

Scalpers and vendors were everywhere, but none were overly aggressive, and strangely, their presence added to the atmosphere. As did music spilling out of the restaurants they passed and the friendly smiles of those, like them, headed to the stadium.

The walk went quickly. Hannah couldn't believe it when they drew close to Camden Yards.

"That's Babe Ruth." Hannah pointed to the statue. "What's he doing here? Babe didn't play for the O's."

"Actually, he did." Charlie gazed admiringly at the bronze statue of the man known as the Great Bambino. "Not only was Babe born in Baltimore, he signed his first official baseball contract with the Orioles. They were a minor-league club at the time."

"Huh, I learned something new."

"The statue is an excellent likeness, but look closely," Charlie urged. "Do you see the error?"

Narrowing her gaze, Hannah studied Babe. His left hand rested on the top of a bat, and his right held a fielder's glove. After a minute, she admitted defeat.

"That's a right-handed fielder's glove. Babe was left-handed." Charlie flashed a smile. "Another bit of trivia."

"I love it." She gazed at him. Her smile faltered when their gazes locked.

"I don't mean to interrupt." A man stepped forward, holding out his phone. "Would one of you mind taking a quick picture of me and my son in front of the statue?"

The boy standing beside his dad looked to be around eleven. Both wore Orioles jerseys and team ball caps.

"Happy to." Charlie reached out and took the phone, doing several bursts. When he handed the man his phone, he pulled his own from his pocket. "Would you mind taking ours?"

"Not at all."

Hannah moved to stand beside Charlie in front of Babe. When the man motioned for them to stand closer, it seemed natural for Charlie to sling an arm around her shoulders.

"I got some great shots." The man handed Charlie's phone back to him.

"Thank you," the boy said in response to his father's sideways glance.

Charlie grinned. "My pleasure."

"You know what I like about Maryland? Everyone is so friendly and so nice," Hannah told Charlie as the father and son strode off, and Charlie pocketed his phone.

"I feel the same." He placed his palm against her back as they made their way to the lower concourse. "That's part of the reason, other than for college, I've never left."

Hannah knew the other part of the reason was his mother.

At the gate, the usher took their tickets, and they entered the passage that separated the warehouse from the stadium.

In minutes, they were surrounded by more orange and black than she'd ever seen in one place. The delicious smell of barbecue from Boog's BBQ teased her nostrils and set her stomach to growling.

"There's really no reason to get to our seats right now, unless that's what you want." Charlie gestured with one hand. "We could grab a beer and inhale the atmosphere."

"I'd love that." Hannah tried to pay for her own, but Charlie was faster.

As she wrapped her fingers around the cup, she gave him a glinting glance. "I'm paying for the hot dogs."

He arched a brow. "We're eating?"

Hannah paused. She'd never considered he might have eaten lunch. And why hadn't she? They hadn't left GraceTown until one. Well, he might not need to eat, but she was going to grab something. It would be a long time before dinner.

"Just kidding." He grinned. "No way am I leaving here without a hot dog and Old Bay fries."

They each got a hot dog and split the fries.

"I missed these." Hannah took a couple of fries from the bag as they walked. "I tried describing the taste once to Emma, and the best I could do was a mixture of sweet, salty and spicy."

"Nothing compares." Charlie licked some of the seasoning from his thumb.

Hannah's heart quickened as she watched, unable to tear her gaze from his mouth.

Obviously feeling her eyes on him, Charlie grabbed a napkin from the sack. "Sorry about that."

"No sorry about it. These are finger-lickin' good." As if to illustrate, Hannah snatched the last fry, popped it into her mouth, then delicately licked the Old Bay seasoning from the tips of her fingers.

When Charlie's gaze remained riveted on her mouth, Hannah knew the hunger in his eyes wasn't from lack of food.

She was the first to break the connection. "Let's check out our seats."

"They're behind left field." Charlie spoke in a hearty tone, gesturing with his head. "This way."

With the sky overhead a brilliant blue and the sun shining down on a field of vivid green, it was a perfect day for baseball. Hannah couldn't stop smiling. She gave Charlie's arm a squeeze. "I'm so glad we came. Thanks for inviting me."

He smiled back. "It was my pleasure."

During the National Anthem, they rose, and Hannah found herself yelling "O" with extra gusto along with Charlie and thousands of fellow fans.

By the time the first pitch was thrown, Hannah was fully into the experience. She shouted with delight at the top of the eighth inning when, with the game tied at 4-4, a sacrifice fly to deep right brought an Orioles player home and gave the O's the lead for the first time.

When the game ended in a 5-4 Orioles victory, Hannah stood and cheered loudly as the team left the field.

Clasping her hands together, she turned to Charlie. "Thank you again."

"Don't thank me." He grinned back at her. "I'm having as much fun as you."

"What's next?" she asked as they filed out of the stadium with everyone else.

"Dinner?" He inclined his head. "Unless you're not hungry after—"

"The hot dog and fries were hours ago." She wrapped her arm around his and held tight as the exiting crowd threatened to push them apart.

They walked to the Inner Harbor, her arm still wrapped around his. Once there, Hannah found herself mesmerized by the smooth water of the historic seaport, the live music and the abundance of restaurants. "I'd be happy to eat anywhere. You choose."

Rising three stories above the Inner Harbor Marina, the Rusty Scupper, a contemporary seafood restaurant, surprised and delighted Hannah from the moment she and Charlie stepped through the doors.

She wasn't sure what pleased her most—the background piano music, the tables with incredible harbor views covered in linen or the amazing food and attentive service.

Hannah might have felt out of place because of how casually she was dressed, but most of the other patrons were dressed in Orioles gear.

It was over an appetizer of calamari that talk turned to the pink house.

"Does it concern you that you haven't seen Maisie since you ran across her in the woods a couple weeks ago?" Charlie sat back in his chair, his hair gleaming like highly polished walnut in the light.

Hannah shook her head. The loose strands of her own hair

tumbled around her shoulders. They'd both taken off their caps when they'd entered the restaurant. She'd also removed the band holding her hair in a tail.

"Remember I didn't actually run across her. She came looking for me." The distinction was important and should be clear, but in case it wasn't, Hannah added, "She can find me anytime. Maisie assured me she'll see me again."

"When do you think that will be?"

"Whenever I need her."

Puzzlement blanketed Charlie's face. "You gotta explain that one."

Hannah thought about telling him that first she needed to figure it out herself. Then it struck her. "When I first ran across Maisie at the pink house, I didn't approach. I didn't want to be a bother. I'd felt that way a lot after Brian's death. Like I needed to soldier on alone and not bother friends who'd already done so much for me."

She paused to take a sip of wine.

"Go on," Charlie urged.

"The next time I saw the house, I was ready to take a chance." Hannah gave a little laugh. "The worst that could happen was she'd toss me off her porch."

Charlie's lips quirked upward. "She didn't."

"No, she didn't. She gave me the letter." Hannah met Charlie's gaze. "I shared the contents with you."

"Because I was Brian's closest friend, and you sensed I'd understand." Charlie lifted a hand and subtly motioned away a waiter headed their way, undoubtedly intending to ensure nothing was wrong with the calamari they'd barely touched.

"The fact that you were Brian's friend was part of it, but not all." Hannah absently picked up a piece of the crispy calamari and dipped it into the red sauce. "By showing you the letter, I opened myself and my world to someone new. My life was changing. I was changing."

Charlie gave a cautious nod. "I can see that."

"Having Maisie come up to me unexpectedly when I was in the woods, well, that reassured me that I'm as important to her as she is to me."

Charlie's gaze never left her face. "Important how?"

"I don't know." Hannah gave a little laugh. "All I know is that when I was a little girl, my imaginary pink house had everything I needed. I'm starting to believe this pink house might, too."

Before he could ask any more questions, Hannah shifted the focus to baseball. "Why did some fans boo when the pitcher's ball went way high? I'm sure he didn't mean to throw a bad pitch."

Nearly two hours later, all Hannah's baseball questions had been patiently answered, and her stomach was very happy. She took a sip of wine and sighed. "Heaven has to be like this."

Charlie, who'd settled for club soda since he was driving, took a long sip, a smile tipping his lips. "Which part of 'this' are you referring to?"

"Everything." Hannah flung out both hands. "The convertible, the ball game and this amazing food. I have never had better seared scallops. For that to mean something, you need to know that I consider myself to be a scallop connoisseur. I also have to say the bite you gave me of your crab-stuffed shrimp was incredible."

"It was tasty," Charlie agreed, appearing amused by her exuberance.

"Next time we come here, that's what I'm getting," she told him. Only after the words had left her mouth did she realize she'd made an assumption that there would be another time. With him.

Before she could backtrack, he spoke. "Sounds like a plan. The server asked if we wanted any dessert. What say you?"

She brought a finger to her lips. "Not ten minutes ago, I swore I couldn't eat another bite, but—"

"The warm butter cake with ice cream could be considered research." He flashed her a devilish smile. "We could split it?"

Hannah grinned. "You've got yourself a deal."

By the time Charlie pulled into her driveway, Hannah was seized with mixed emotions. Though she'd been up early baking, and the day had been a long one, she wasn't ready for her time with Charlie to end.

She shifted in her seat to face him. "I don't know about you, but this has been a top-ten day for me."

"It isn't over yet." Charlie pushed open the car door and stepped out. "There's still the walk to your front door."

"A gentleman to the core."

"I try."

When he opened her car door and offered his hand, she took it.

The surge of electricity when her flesh met his had her inhaling sharply. Instead of releasing her hand once she was out of the car, he held it as they climbed the steps to her porch.

When they reached the front door, she turned to him. "Seriously, thank you for an amazing, marvelous day."

He brushed a strand of hair back from her face with the tip of one finger. "Seriously, it was my pleasure."

She knew he was going to kiss her. Knew it as well as she knew her own name. She tipped her face up to his.

For a second, just a split second, he hesitated. Then his mouth closed over hers.

This kiss was nothing like the brief brushes of lips they'd shared before. While this might have started out as a gentle melding of mouths, when his arms slid around her and her fingers tangled in his hair, the kiss went from zero to sixty in a heartbeat.

The heat that flowed through her veins was jet-fuel hot. His kisses didn't so much devour as consume. Want and need that she'd thought had been buried with Brian had her wanting to pull Charlie inside and tear off his clothes.

*Brian.*

Hannah jerked back, her breath coming in short puffs. She resisted the urge to touch her tingling lips. "Good night, Charlie."

His dark eyes turned watchful. "Everything okay?"

She offered what she hoped was a bright smile. "Everything is wonderful."

"Okay, then." Shoving his hands into his pockets, he rocked back on his heels. "I'll see you tomorrow."

"Yes, see you tomorrow." She waited until he stepped off the porch before slipping inside.

# CHAPTER TWENTY

That night, Hannah dreamed. She was standing in a field enjoying the sun on her face when she spotted a man in the distance walking toward her. As he drew close, her heart flip-flopped. Joy, rich and lush, flooded her.

She took off running, stumbling in her rush to reach him.

When she drew close, his expression brightened in welcome. A feeling of rightness stole over her as she slid into his arms. Here he was. Here he was.

But when Hannah lifted her face to him and his lips closed over hers, she realized it was Charlie she kissed, not Brian. Charlie who held her tightly against his chest as if he never wanted to let her go. Charlie who tenderly stroked her hair.

Hannah woke with a start, her heart racing. Though she told herself it was only a dream, the intense feelings lingered.

Swiping at her damp cheeks, she sat up in bed, yearning for the moment in her dream when Charlie's arms had wrapped around her, and everything in her world had felt right.

Then guilt rushed in, swamping her. She'd loved Brian as much as it was possible to love a person. So, how, after only a year, could she be having these kinds of feelings for someone else?

Pushing the troubling question aside, Hannah slipped out of bed. Getting more sleep wasn't going to happen. Not the way her insides churned.

After making coffee and downing a cup, Hannah pulled on her running shorts and top. Streetlights cast their golden glow on the quiet neighborhood as she took off down the sidewalk.

Charlie's house was dark. Not surprising, as the sun was only the faintest glimmer in the east. What was surprising was her being awake and running before dawn.

Hannah veered into the street when Hugh's underground sprinklers kicked on, then jolted when a black cat streaked in front of her, likely on its way home after a night of prowling.

Focusing on the sounds around her helped her settle. Running shoes striking the pavement. The *tsk-tsk-tsk* of Hugh's sprinklers. The soothing sounds of a dove perched high in a tree.

Hannah found her stride at mile two, and her thoughts returned to Charlie and the feel of his mouth against hers.

He brought the desire she'd thought had died with Brian surging back with a vengeance. But her need for her neighbor went far beyond the physical.

Charlie was a good man. She respected him as a person and enjoyed his company. When she was with him, there was none of the awkwardness she experienced around other men. For whatever reason, they just fit.

Was it too soon? Could she really be falling in love with her husband's best friend?

Shoving aside questions that appeared to have no answer, Hannah made the loop that would take her back home. Though this morning she felt as if she could go for hours, she wasn't in shape for a long run.

She slowed to a walk when she reached the neighborhood,

and as she walked, streetlights winked off while lights in various homes flipped on.

Charlie's home was one of the houses now sporting lights. She wondered as she walked by if it was him who was up, or Lisa. Or maybe they both were.

Once she returned home, she went to the kitchen, intending to do some experimental baking, but her heart wasn't in it.

All she could think about was the dream and her feelings for Charlie.

On Thursday, Lisa looked up from her computer when Charlie dropped market bags on the counter. She'd moved into the kitchen by the time he came in with the rest of the bags.

"What is all this?" She chuckled and gestured to the cluttered counter. "Are we having a dinner party I don't know about?"

Charlie paused, his hand on the fresh linguine noodles. "I thought I'd make dinner for Hannah tomorrow. She loves seafood, so I'm using your recipe, the one with pasta, lemon and herbs?"

"I know the one."

Conscious of his mother's steady gaze, Charlie continued to put away the groceries. He lifted the asparagus that he planned to bake, spritz with lemon, then top with melted Parmesan cheese shavings.

His lips curved as he thought how surprised Hannah would be by the feast he had planned for her. She had no idea he was more than a passable cook. They still had so much to learn about each other.

That's what porch talks were for. Since the baseball game last weekend, he and Hannah had continued their nightly tradition of conversation and wine. But there had been no more kissing.

Charlie hadn't pushed. This relationship—and that's what it

was, whether either of them wanted to admit it or not—was already moving at warp speed.

While he was determined to give her the time and space she needed, he hoped this dinner would show her just how much she mattered to him.

Lisa took a seat at the table. She cleared her throat. "You know I like Hannah."

Unease coursed up his spine as Charlie faced his mom. Going for casual, he rested his back against the counter. "I like her, too."

"Brian hasn't been gone that long." His mother's brows pulled together, and Charlie could see her carefully considering her words. "I don't know that it's a good idea for you and Hannah to be spending so much time together."

"That doesn't make sense." With great effort, Charlie kept his voice even. "You told me when she moved here that we have to be good neighbors and friends to her."

"Planning elaborate dinners and convertible rides go beyond being good friends and neighbors." Pushing to her feet, Lisa steadied herself, then crossed to him. She placed a gentle hand on his arm. "You like her as more than a friend, Charlie. If it's not apparent to her, it certainly is to me."

Charlie couldn't deny his growing feelings for Hannah. He wasn't sure why he would even try. He wanted to ask his mother if she saw that same evidence of those growing feelings when she looked at Hannah, but he wasn't sure he wanted to hear the answer.

Though he knew Hannah liked him as a friend and enjoyed his company, he wanted more. But Brian had been his friend. He wouldn't disrespect his memory by pushing his widow for more than she was ready to give.

Charlie only wished he knew when she'd be ready. If she'd ever be ready.

The sound of his mother clearing her throat had Charlie pulling his thoughts back to their conversation.

"I enjoy being with Hannah. I believe she enjoys being with me." Charlie met his mother's direct gaze with an equally direct one of his own. "Would I like more? Yes. Absolutely. But if and when we move forward, that will be her decision, not mine."

"I just don't want to see either of you hurt." His mother's gaze took in the groceries. "I spoke with Hannah earlier today. She didn't mention coming for dinner tomorrow. It might be a good idea to ask Hannah if she's interested before you go to all this work."

*Interested.*

The word struck at the heart of Charlie's fears. Hannah had to be interested. Hadn't she told him that last Saturday's trip to Camden Yards was a top-ten day? Hadn't they kissed until they'd both been dizzy?

"You're right." He pulled out his phone. "I'll do that right now."

A minute later, Charlie dropped into a chair, leaving food still in bags on the counter.

His mother, who'd remained silent during the call, cast him a sympathetic look and took a seat across the table.

Charlie's lips lifted in a sardonic smile. "Go ahead. Say 'I told you so.'"

"Why would I do that?"

"Because you know Hannah turned me down." Charlie expelled a breath. "She already has dinner plans. Tomorrow is her and Brian's anniversary."

A look of surprise briefly widened his mother's eyes. "Who is she going to dinner with?"

"No one." Charlie frowned, trying to recall the exact words she'd used. "At least I don't think so. Hannah said it was their anniversary, and she was having dinner at Normandy to recognize the date. I can't figure out what she's doing."

Lisa placed her folded hands on the table. She met Charlie's troubled gaze with a calm one of her own. "This might sound strange, but I have more concerns about you than I do about her."

Everything in Charlie stilled. "What are you saying?"

"Up to this point, you've been more of a live-in-the-moment kind of guy. All your relationships have been simple, uncomplicated and short-lived."

"None of those women were right." For the life of him, Charlie couldn't figure out what his mother was getting at. "Why would I keep dating a woman when I know she isn't what I want, what I need? That wouldn't be fair."

"I agree." His mother pinned him with her gaze. "Which is why I think it's time for you to take a step back and ask yourself if you're the kind of man Hannah needs."

On Friday, Hannah dressed with care for dinner. Her black sheath was one she hadn't worn since last year. She added the single strand of pearls Brian had given her for her twenty-fifth birthday.

That celebration felt like a lifetime ago. The hair she normally let hang loose now boasted a half-up style that Brian had told her made her look sophisticated, but approachable.

Hannah thought the pearls and hair both added to the formal look of her evening's attire. She'd also taken extra time with her makeup, adding shadow, eyeliner and mascara to make her eyes look large and mysterious.

For most of the day, she'd warred with herself over whether to keep or cancel tonight's plans. In the end, she let the reservation stand. Though he'd done a good job of hiding it when she'd mentioned her plan for tonight to Charlie, she'd heard the shock in his voice.

Based on his reaction, she decided not to tell Emma or Mackenna. Hannah could guess how they'd respond. Understandable, since neither had lost a spouse. For all his peculiarities, her father might be the only one who would truly understand where she was coming from.

Looking in the mirror one more time, Hannah studied herself with a critical eye. After a second, she added more color to her lips, smiling as she remembered how much Brian had loved kissing the coral smoothness off her mouth at the end of an evening out.

Her smile faded.

She really hoped tonight wasn't a mistake.

Hannah arrived at the elegant French restaurant ten minutes before her reservation. The last time she'd been at Normandy had been the night of her high school graduation. She didn't recall the restaurant being particularly romantic, but then, well, she'd been with her father.

Tonight, the atmosphere at Normandy, with its hushed elegance, fresh flower arrangements and enticing scents, brought tears to Hannah's eyes. This was the perfect venue for an anniversary dinner.

Blinking back the unexpected moisture flooding her eyes, Hannah stepped to the hostess stand and came face-to-face with Ashleigh Christopher, who was on the phone finishing up taking a reservation.

Recognition flashed in the schoolteacher's eyes as she hung up. "Hannah. This is a surprise. Is Charlie with you?"

"No." Hannah tightened her fingers around her beaded clutch. "The reservation is under Danbury."

A speculative gleam filled Ashleigh's eyes. Hannah braced herself for questions, but another couple's arrival had Ashleigh motioning to a young man who stood nearby. "Edward, please escort Ms. Danbury to table fifteen."

"This way, ma'am."

In this instance, Hannah didn't mind being called *ma'am* by a young man only a handful of years her junior. When he stopped by a table in clear view of the hostess stand, she demurred. "Do you have something farther back?"

"Yes, ma'am." He didn't miss a beat. "Please follow me."

This time when he paused beside a table for two, she nodded her approval and returned his smile. "This will do nicely. Thank you for being so accommodating."

"My pleasure." He pulled out her chair, lifted the napkin at her place setting and set it on her lap. "Your waiter will be right with you. Bon appétit."

The waiter arrived with the bottle of Cristal that Hannah had preordered, along with two glasses. He inclined his head. "Would you prefer to wait until your companion arrives before—"

"No," Hannah cut him off. "I'd like a glass now."

"As you wish." The waiter, an older man in his fifties with a Van Dyke beard and sharp eyes, kept his expression bland as he uncorked the bottle and poured her a glass.

"I'll wait a bit to order," she told him. "I'll signal you when I'm ready."

Taking a sip of champagne, Hannah gazed at the empty chair. She pictured Brian smiling back at her from across the table, looking so handsome in his dark suit and favorite Hermes red tie. Saw him listening attentively to her update on Hannah Cakes and her home renovations. Felt the warmth of his smile as she relayed the details of the Camden Yards trip.

He'd be happy for her. Happy how she was handling all the changes in her life. She gave a decisive nod. Yes, he'd be happy. All Brian had ever wanted was for her to be happy.

Hannah signaled the waiter, told him she'd be eating alone and ordered. Lamb brochette had been her and Brian's favorite meal to order at Republique in Greensboro. It seemed an appropriate choice for tonight.

Though Hannah hadn't eaten since early this morning, she

had to force herself through each course, barely tasting the excellent food. She wondered if Charlie liked lamb, wondered if he'd have encouraged her to try something she'd never had before if he were here.

Despite the fact that she'd barely touched her meal, Hannah ordered a slice of opera cake to take home with her.

Brian loved dessert, especially cake. Hannah tightened her fingers around the white bakery box and expelled a shuddering breath.

Ashleigh was busy with customers, so Hannah thankfully was spared the need to deal with her as she hurried out the door.

Emma had once told her time was a gift.

Was she squandering that gift by holding on so tightly to Brian? But would moving on mean she had to forget him?

If it did, that was something she absolutely could not do.

# CHAPTER TWENTY-ONE

From the spot on his front step, Charlie watched a silver Prius pull into Hannah's driveway, Hannah in the back seat.

Even after the Uber drove off, she remained at the edge of the walkway leading to her porch, a white bakery box in her hands.

Framed as she was in the porchlight, Charlie saw that she wore a sleek black dress, shiny black heels and pearls. She was the picture of elegance and beauty. That might be what everyone saw at first glance, but Charlie had learned that there was far more to Hannah than a pretty face and killer body.

She remained where she was, making no effort to head inside. Unable to sit any longer, Charlie pushed to his feet. In a flash, he was crossing the lawn that separated them.

Though a tiny warning light flashed red in his head, telling Charlie to proceed with caution, he moved quickly. She looked so sad and lost standing there.

Whatever she needed, he would provide. If he could cheer her up or comfort her in some way, that's what he would do.

If Hannah was aware of his approach, she didn't show it. Her gaze remained riveted on the rosebush she'd planted not long after she moved in.

He inhaled deeply. The scent from the roses mingled with her clean, citrusy fragrance.

"You look lovely." Charlie kept his voice soft, not wanting to startle her.

She spun to face him. Her brows drew together. "What did you say?"

"I said you look lovely." Charlie gestured with one hand. "I don't believe I've seen you all dressed up before. You clean up good."

His attempt to inject a little levity fell flat.

Hannah's gaze dropped as if she needed to remind herself what she wore before she lifted one hand to her pearls. "Thank you. Brian gave me these for my twenty-fifth birthday. Today would have been our tenth anniversary."

"Right. You mentioned—"

"Why are you here?"

"I saw you come home and—"

"What do you want, Charlie?"

Her words, spoken in such a matter-of-fact tone, startled Charlie almost as much as the coolness that filled her eyes. She'd already turned to climb the steps to her porch by the time he found his voice.

"What's going on, Hannah?" He gentled his tone, speaking to her back as he followed her up the porch steps. "Have I done something to offend you?"

Charlie hoped he'd misread the situation. Hoped she would say it wasn't him and explain.

When she dropped into one of the wicker chairs, he pulled the other one close and sat down.

A startled look crossed her face, as if she hadn't expected him to follow her. In fact, she was looking at him as if she didn't want him there.

Panic tried to rise, but Charlie shoved it down. Something had clearly upset her. Once she told him what was troubling her, she'd feel better, and everything between them would be back to normal.

He gestured to the box she clutched in her lap and kept his voice light, Even managed to add a smile. "What do you have in there?"

"French opera cake. It was Brian's favorite."

The sadness in her eyes tugged at his heart. He thought about telling her he missed Brian, too, but refrained. Just like he stopped himself from reaching over and covering her hand with his.

"French opera cake, huh? I don't even know what that is. I bet it's good."

Instead of explaining, as he'd expected, Hannah met his gaze, and he felt as if she was seeing him clearly for the first time since he'd sat down. "You've been very helpful to me in coping with my loss of Brian."

It wasn't so much what she said as the way she said it. Thinking of yesterday's conversation with his mother, Charlie hesitated. Could it be that he'd misread the situation? That while he was falling in love with her, she was only working through Brian's loss? The thought drew blood. *No. No. No.*

Hannah cared about him. He knew she did.

"What are you saying, Hannah?" He made sure his voice gave away none of his inner turmoil.

"We can be friends." She met his gaze with an unyielding one of her own. "As far as being more—"

"I was training wheels." He spoke without thinking, trying to process what was happening as his heart split in two.

"Pardon?" Her brows pulled together in obvious confusion. For the first time, he noticed the lines of fatigue and strain edging her eyes.

Emotion flooded his brain. "I was your test run. While I was developing feelings for you, you were just using me like training wheels to see what life might look like post-Brian.

After all, good old Charlie was safe, since you never much cared for me anyway." Charlie shoved to his feet. "Glad I could be of help."

"That's not what I—" Hannah surged to her feet so quickly that the box tumbled to her feet and split open, sending bits of cake flying.

She cried out in frustration, but Charlie paid no heed as he got out of there as fast as he could.

~

Hannah spent the weekend cleaning her house...and missing Charlie.

She hadn't seen him since he'd stormed off her porch on Friday night. The end of their burgeoning relationship was for the best, she told herself, though she couldn't quite make herself believe it.

On the ride home from Normandy, she hadn't been able to stop thinking about Brian. If she loved him even half as much as she thought she did, how could she be having these intense feelings for Charlie so soon?

The cake had cinched it. On the ride home, she'd found herself thinking how nice it would be if Charlie stopped over so they could enjoy the cake together with a glass of wine.

It hit her that she was actually considering splitting Brian's cake with Charlie. On their anniversary.

A triumphant shout from outside had her moving to her window, where she saw Charlie exchange a high five with Sean. At the feet of the two men, surrounded by tools, a lawnmower was running smoothly.

Hannah was unprepared for the wave of longing that washed over her. She reminded herself that she'd told him they could be friends.

Hannah rubbed the bridge of her nose, remembering the look

on his face when she'd said that. She'd hurt him. That had never been her intent.

The ringing of her phone startled her. Mackenna's ring tone—an obnoxious voice shouting, "Answer me!"—must have carried through the open window, because Charlie abruptly turned.

For a second, their eyes met and held.

Before she could smile or even lift a hand in greeting, Charlie bent down and began picking up tools.

Taking a quick step out of view, Hannah answered the phone. "I definitely have to get a new ring tone for you. This one is obnoxious."

Mackenna laughed. "It's a good thing I prefer to text."

True. Which made her calling now—and during a workday—puzzling.

"It's always good to hear from you," Hannah assured her friend.

"Listen, I only have a sec. Jace's cousin will be in town on Friday. Jace mentioned maybe the four of us could go out." Mackenna's tone turned persuasive. "His cousin is an attorney specializing in small businesses, so the two of you should have lots to talk about. Jace says he's super nice. Divorced. No kids. Please say you'll do it."

"I'm afraid Friday won't work—"

That's all she got out before Mackenna interrupted. "I knew it. I told Jace that you and Charlie probably already have plans. He knew you'd come to Skyline Farm together, but he didn't realize all the other stuff you'd been doing."

The last thing Hannah wanted to do was go out with Jace's cousin. Would there really be any harm in letting Mackenna think she had a date with Charlie on Friday? Mackenna would certainly accept that excuse more readily than Hannah simply saying no.

Hannah shoved aside the temptation. She wouldn't lie to her friend. "Charlie and I were seeing a lot of each other, but..."

She paused, searching for the perfect explanation.

*But we were getting too close, and I got scared.*

*But now it's over.*

*But he doesn't even want to be my friend now.*

"That's okay. I totally understand. Duty calls. Chat soon. Tell Charlie hi."

Sighing, Hannah pocketed the phone, then slanted a look at her open laptop. All morning, she'd tried to work up a social media plan for Hannah Cakes, but she had made little progress.

Too many thoughts were circling in her head.

She spotted her hiking boots by the back door, and her spirits lifted ever so slightly.

A walk in the woods might be just what she needed to clear her head.

# CHAPTER TWENTY-TWO

Hannah didn't follow the directions she'd saved on her phone for finding the pink house. Even when the tree with the initials carved into the trunk came into view, she didn't turn left.

Why bother? She'd followed those directions so many times, and each time, she had come up empty. Today, she would walk through the woods the way she had that first time. If she ran into the house and Maisie, great. If not, she'd get a good hike, some fresh air and hopefully clear her head.

A bird in a tree called out. The swath of bright red on its wings caught her eye and made her smile. As she followed its flight, her smile faded, and her breath caught in her throat.

She blinked once. Then twice. Still there.

The house, bright pink with gingerbread on the eaves and a spacious porch, was just as she remembered. As she drew closer, she saw Maisie sitting alone on the porch. Setting down the book she'd been reading, Maisie lifted a hand in greeting.

Eagerness fueled Hannah's steps as she hurried closer.

"Good afternoon, Hannah." Maisie stood and smiled warmly, gesturing for Hannah to join her on the porch when she reached the steps. "I had a feeling you might stop by, so I made us something to drink. I hope you like lemonade."

Hannah smiled. "I had a feeling our paths might cross again today."

"You and me." Maisie tapped her temple with a finger. "Same wavelength."

"A love of lemonade is another thing we have in common." Hannah climbed the steps and took a seat in the chair Maisie indicated, relaxing against the back.

How could stepping onto this porch feel so much like home?

Maisie poured lemonade into two glasses with ice. When she leaned close to hand her one of them, the sweet floral fragrance of Maisie's perfume teased Hannah's nostrils. "The first time we introduced ourselves," Maisie said, "I don't believe I told you that I've always loved the name Hannah."

"My mother did, too." Hannah accepted the glass and smiled her thanks. "My dad has always said that when he and my mom were discussing baby names, no other name would do if I was a girl."

Maisie's expression softened. "That's a special memory."

"I didn't really know my mother," Hannah confided. "I don't even have a clear picture of what she looked like."

A startled look crossed Maisie's face. "I know you told me she passed away when you were young, but surely you have a few pictures."

"My father, well, he wasn't himself for a period of time after she died. He put all the pictures together in a shoebox and stored them somewhere safe." Hannah gave a little laugh. "The trouble was, when things did settle down, he couldn't recall the location of that safe spot."

Maisie sipped her lemonade. "He's never remembered where he put them?"

"Nope." Hannah took a drink and felt the last of the tension slip from her shoulders. "Never found them."

"My husband used to do the same, put things away in strange places, then forget where they were." Maisie chuckled. "When we lived in an older home, there was a…hidey-hole, I guess you'd call it, at the far back of our bedroom closet, way at the top. Once I realized he saw that as a safe place to store things, I always looked there first."

"Does your husband live here with you?"

"I've been married twice," Maisie said in response. "Both men were the love of my life."

"Brian was the love of my life." Hannah wondered how she could be having this conversation with a virtual stranger and it not feel odd. "I thought we'd be together forever."

Maisie reached over and patted Hannah's hand, the light touch as soft and soothing as a mother's caress. "I know how much it hurts to lose someone you love. I was only eighteen when I married my Nathaniel. Even though I was young, I knew, just knew, he was the one for me. I didn't realize our time together would be cut so short."

"What happened?"

Maisie's cornflower-blue eyes took on a distant glow. "Car accident. We'd been married less than a year. He was on his way home from work. When I opened the door and saw the sheriff standing there, my heart just stopped. Even before he told me, I knew Nathaniel was gone."

Hannah reached over and squeezed her hand.

Maisie returned the squeeze, then expelled a shaky breath. "The worse day of my life."

"I'm sorry for your loss." Hannah's voice thickened with emotion. "You didn't even have a chance to say good-bye."

"No." Maisie blinked back tears. "I'm glad you and Brian had that chance."

Hannah realized that as difficult as those last few weeks had been, spending that time together had been a gift. "We left nothing unsaid, no matter how difficult it was to talk about."

"I didn't have family nearby, but reaching out to friends afterwards helped." Maisie inclined her head. "I seem to recall you mentioning a friend of Brian's who was helpful."

"Charlie. I didn't connect with him until I moved back to GraceTown. He lives next door to me with his mother." Hannah held up her hand before Maisie could get the wrong idea. "His mother has MS, and they share the house. That way, he can help her as necessary. I'd do the same for mine."

"Would you?" A soft look filled Maisie's eyes.

"Absolutely." Hannah gave a decisive nod.

"Charlie sounds like a wonderful man." Maisie sat back in her seat and eyed Hannah. "Tell me about him."

Hannah didn't really want to talk about Charlie. His absence from her life was still an open wound. But he *had* been a good friend to her, and somehow it seemed important that Maisie know that.

"Charlie is really down-to-earth. By that, I mean he's not into the latest fashions or fancy cars. He likes jeans, T-shirts and his truck." Hannah chuckled. "Though he's very accomplished and super smart, he doesn't feel the need to impress anyone."

Maisie offered an encouraging smile.

Hannah leaned forward. "What makes Charlie special is that he really cares about people. He'd do anything to help me."

"A man like that doesn't come around that often."

"I just wish I knew what to do about him." Hannah sighed. The second the words left her lips, she wished she could pull them back.

What to do about Charlie and her growing feelings for him was something she needed to figure out on her own.

"Forget I said anything." Hannah waved a dismissive hand.

"I've found that sometimes," Maisie said casually, "when I'm struggling to figure out something, it helps to talk things out with someone who has no skin in the game."

Hannah had to smile. *Skin in the game* was a favorite expression of her father. She hadn't heard anyone else say it in a very long time.

Still, what Maisie was saying did make a certain amount of sense.

"I loved Brian with my whole heart. When I stood in front of the congregation on our wedding day and promised to love him forever, I meant every word." Hannah expelled a long breath. "During our marriage, we had our ups and downs, sure, but the love and the commitment to our marriage were always there."

"Now you've started to have feelings for Charlie."

"Yes. I've started to have feelings for Charlie," Hannah admitted. "I'm not sure what to do with them."

"I mentioned I was married before," Maisie said after a long moment.

Hannah gave a cautious nod, not sure where this was headed.

"It wasn't long after Nathaniel died that I met my honey bear." Her lips quirked upward. "He was about as different from Nathaniel as he could be. Nathaniel was fun-loving and carefree with an infectious laugh. Honey bear was serious, focused and driven to provide."

"The name honey bear doesn't seem to fit that personality type." Just saying the nickname had Hannah smiling.

"The thing was, he was also kind, loving and seriously sweet." Maisie's expression turned dreamy. "I adored him, and he adored me."

"How long after Nathaniel's death did you meet him?"

"Six months." Maisie lifted a hand. "I know it was quick, and I wasn't looking for anyone. But my honey bear was so unlike Nathaniel that it didn't occur to me when we started talking that there could be anything more between us than friendship. I guess you could say my guard was down."

"You fell in love with him before you realized it was happening."

Maisie's lips curved, and her eyes shone. "I did."

"Where is he—?"

"Is that what happened with you and Charlie?" Maisie asked. "He snuck under your defenses?"

Hannah glanced away and gave a jerky nod.

Maisie reached over and touched her arm. "It's okay to love again, hon. There is no appropriate timeline, only what's right for you. Don't let anyone tell you differently."

How was it that simply speaking with Maisie helped her sort through her tangled thoughts? Was this what it would have been like to have a mother? Someone to guide and direct, but not push?

"I had friends wanting to fix me up only months after Brian passed away. I wasn't interested. Now, though a year has passed, some will say it's too soon."

"What matters is what you think, what you know in your heart." A rueful smile tipped Maisie's lips. "I even had someone tell me I must not have really loved Nathaniel if I could fall in love with another man so soon."

Hannah hesitated. "Did hearing them say that make you wonder if it was true?"

"No, because I knew in my heart how much I loved Nathaniel." Maisie's eyes grew distant with memories, then she smiled. "My honey bear brought light back into my life. Falling in love again isn't disrespectful to the one who's gone, but a tribute to them. Nathaniel loved me. I know he'd want me to feel joy again."

"Brian told me before he died that he wanted me to be happy."

"There's your answer."

A sudden gust of wind swept through the trees, rattling the table.

Maisie looked up at the sky and stood. "A storm is coming. You better head home."

Hannah rose, reluctant to leave.

She wasn't sure what to think when Maisie stepped close and

wrapped her arms around her, the sweet fragrance of lilies enveloping her.

"I'm so glad we had this chance to get better acquainted. You're a wonderful woman, Hannah, a woman any mother would be proud of." Maisie brushed her lips against Hannah's hair. "Be happy, my sweet girl."

Hannah hesitated. "When will I see you again?"

"I'll never be far away. Now, hurry home." Maisie gestured. "This isn't the place for you."

As the wind continued to blow and distant thunder rumbled, Hannah rushed down the steps.

When she turned back, Maisie was gone. The woman had been right. The porch wasn't the place for either of them. Not now.

# CHAPTER TWENTY-THREE

Hoping to beat the downpour, Hannah ran the last block to her house. Unfortunately, by the time she could reach her porch, the rain began to fall in sheets, soaking her to the bone. Stripping out of her clothes, she headed to the bathroom for a quick shower.

The water, so warm and soothing against her chilled skin, had her lingering under the spray while her mind drifted to her conversation with Maisie in the woods.

What the woman had said made sense. There shouldn't be a timeline for how quickly or slowly someone moved into a new relationship after losing a spouse. So many factors were involved.

Once she finally left the warmth of the shower, Hannah spent the rest of the day experimenting with her own version of an opera cake. The one she'd brought home from Normandy had been the classic six-layer French cake featuring joconde sponge and chocolate ganache, topped with a coffee buttercream frosting.

Today, Hannah made the recipe her own, brushing an almond sponge cake with coffee-flavored syrup and adding instant espresso powder to the frosting. Now that the cake was assembled and chilling in the refrigerator, she headed upstairs to the small room her mother had used for sewing.

Over the years, Hannah and her father had utilized every room in the house except for one. Her dad had made it very clear that as long as he lived there, that room was off-limits.

Which was why the room looked exactly as it had the day her mother died. A shelving unit above the table held her mother's sewing supplies and swatches of fabrics. A half-finished dress next to the machine and racks that her dad must have mounted held everything from thread bobbins to ribbon spools.

Planning to turn the small room into a home office, Hannah made quick work of clearing out the room. All that was left was to empty the closet.

She'd left one item hanging in there, a red-and-white gingham apron with cross-stitching on the pockets. The knowledge that this had been her mother's apron had Hannah holding it to her cheek for several seconds before putting it back on the hanger. She would keep the apron, and every time she wore it, she would think of her mother.

Hannah told herself the faint lily-of-the-valley scent in the closet had to be coming from the mounds of carefully folded fabric stored on the top shelf.

Even standing on her tiptoes, Hannah couldn't reach the fabric. Grabbing a step stool, she climbed to the top step and began dropping fabric into an open cardboard box.

The last pile of fabric made a satisfying thud when it landed on top of a floral print. Ready to climb down, Hannah paused. A tarnished round pull, flat against the back of the empty shelf, caught her eye.

Hannah narrowed her gaze, then inhaled sharply.

It was a hidey-hole. Like the one Maisie had mentioned from her own house.

Excitement surged as Hannah imagined the treasures she might find inside. Leaning forward, she slipped her fingers around the ring and pulled. It took a second tug with more force to have the drawer sliding out.

Her heart beat an erratic rhythm as she picked up the surprisingly light drawer. Taking the drawer downstairs, she placed it carefully on the kitchen table.

When she opened the top, her breath quickened at the sight of the shoebox inside.

Anticipation fueled her movements, making her clumsy as she lifted out the shoebox. Pictures of every shape and size spilled out onto the table, photos of her as a baby, photos of her dad as young man and...photos of a beautiful woman with golden hair.

Hannah recognized her instantly.

With trembling fingers, she flipped over the photograph to see that her father had written in his scrupulously precise penmanship the words *Charlotte Mae Beahr. My beloved Maisie.*

Tears slipped down Hannah's cheeks. How could this be? Then again, it explained so much.

The closeness Hannah had felt with the woman. The pink house from her childhood that had held everything she wanted, including a mother.

Even the letter from Brian that Maisie had given her. A gift from beyond the grave. A reminder that the past and the present weren't separate, but were intertwined.

Whether or not she could remember her mother, her mother was a part of her even now. Just like Brian was.

Hannah glanced at the envelope she'd left on the kitchen table, the one Maisie had given her from Brian.

Setting down the picture of her mother, Hannah picked up the envelope. She didn't have to do things that Brian had loved to do in order to remember him or prove she loved him. She just had to keep living, keep loving, keep being happy, because that was at the heart of their bond.

*The future is not guaranteed.*

*I want you to be happy.*

Those two simple phrases urged her to not take time for granted, reminding her that life was fleeting, and no one was promised tomorrow.

Hannah realized it would have been okay if Charlie had sat on the porch with her Saturday night, sharing cake and conversation.

Brian wouldn't have begrudged her pursuing a relationship with Charlie. He'd known his best friend was a stand-up guy, a good man who could be trusted with her heart.

With great reverence, Hannah laid Brian's letter on top of the photographs and closed the lid.

Then she took the drawer back upstairs and put it back where she'd found it.

These were her memories to revisit as often as she wanted. Unlike her father, she wouldn't forget where to find them.

Hannah barreled out the back door and straight into a broad chest.

Strong hands grabbed her shoulders to steady her, then immediately dropped away.

"Hannah."

"Charlie."

They both spoke at the same time. "I was—"

Hannah laughed.

"You go first," he said.

"I was on my way to see you."

The smile that never failed to make her heart beat faster lifted his lips. "Funny thing. I was coming to see you."

She tapped her temple with her index finger, her gaze never leaving his face. "Same wavelength."

"I hope so." Appearing suddenly unsure, he shifted from one foot to the other. "Hannah, I—"

"I know it's early, but can I interest you in a piece of cake and some wine?"

A watchful look filled his eyes. "Sure."

"You sit. I'll be back in a sec." Certain now, so very sure of the course she was about to take, Hannah went into the kitchen, cut two thin slices of cake, filled two glasses with a sparkling white Bordeaux she'd been wanting to try and put it all on a tray.

Charlie was waiting on the other side of the screen door. Pulling it open when she approached, he lifted the tray from her hands. "I've got this."

Once he set the tray on the table between the two wicker chairs, he waited for her to sit before he did.

"I want to say I'm sorry for how I behaved the other night," he said, shifting to more fully face her. "I read too much into a few outings and a few kisses. You never told me you wanted more. That was my hope, but that's on me, not you."

"I want more."

Confusion flickered across his face. "You said you want to be friends. You made it clear that was all you wanted."

Hannah surged to her feet, unable to sit. She moved to the porch rail and stared in the direction of the woods. "This has been a confusing year for me. Since Brian's death, it's been two steps forward, one step back in terms of my emotions."

"I didn't mean to pressure you—"

He stood beside her now, and she reached over and gave his hand a squeeze. "You didn't. I enjoyed our time together immensely. I liked getting to know you. When I found myself enjoying my time with you so much, I started feeling guilty, as if I was being somehow disloyal, as if I hadn't loved Brian as much as I thought I had."

"I experienced some of that guilt, too." Charlie blew out a breath. "Brian was my friend, my best friend from as far back as I can remember. Having these kinds of feelings for his wife—"

Hannah tightened her grip on his hand. "I know Brian meant

what he said in the letter. He wants me to be happy. I know in my heart he'd want the same for you."

"What are you saying, Hannah?"

"I'm saying I'd like us to continue to explore a relationship." Hannah spoke deliberately, the words coming straight from her heart. "I'm saying let's keep moving forward."

"As friends?" His intense gaze remained riveted on her face.

"If that's all you want. I'd like more." She offered a tentative smile. "This time we've been given is a gift. I don't want to squander it. I say let's enjoy cake, conversation and maybe a ride in a sporty convertible every now and then and see where we end up."

"You've got a deal. We could shake on it, but I have a better idea." With a smile, Charlie tugged her to him and closed his mouth over hers.

Just one more thing to love about Charlie Rogan, Hannah thought, right before she lost herself in his kiss.

He knew the value of embracing the moment.

I hope you enjoyed Hannah's story. Losing my own mother left a hole inside me. There are so many times after her death I found myself wanting to pick up the phone and call her. Sometimes to simply chat, other times to ask her advice. I comfort myself that at least I had her through my growing up years.

Hannah wasn't that fortunate. But I truly believe a mother's love never dies, which is what led me to write this story. The Pink House? Well, when my daughter was little she had a Pink House (an imaginary one that had everything she ever wanted) When I was conceiving this story, I found myself thinking what would Hannah want that Pink House to contain...

By now you probably have guessed that there's something

about GraceTown (named by my eldest granddaughter Grace) where magical things happen.

If you loved this story, you're going to adore The Love Token, the next book in the series. Order your copy now or keep reading for a sneak peek:

# SNEAK PEEK OF THE LOVE TOKEN

## Chapter One

"You look positively mah-velous, darling."

Sophia Jessup's lips curved at the compliment. After taking a second to adjust her straw hat, she turned from her reflection in the antique beveled mirror and smiled at the woman in the doorway to Timeless Treasures.

Standing nearly six feet tall, Ruby Osentowski—Sophie's bestie and second-in-command here at the store—was known for her quick wit and eclectic fashion sense.

Today, wearing a midi boho-chic caftan with an ostrich feather imprint, Ruby definitely drew the eye. Reacting to the humidity that was GraceTown, Maryland, in the summer, Ruby's brown hair exploded around her pretty face in a riot of curls.

"What are you doing here already?" Sophie feigned confusion. "You aren't due in for another hour."

"And you're not supposed to be here at all. But I knew I'd find you here. Just like you knew I'd be early." With a smug smile, Ruby strode down the center aisle toward Sophie, passing a display of mechanical coin banks and artfully arranged vintage cereal boxes.

When she reached the back sales counter, Ruby handed Sophie a cup from Perkatory, a coffee shop down the block, before calling out, "Andrew, I brought coffee."

Andrew Doman, college student and part-time employee for the last year, appeared from the back. Tall with a mop of brown hair, he sported black-rimmed glasses that had a habit of sliding down his nose.

Crossing to them, he picked up the cup Ruby had set on the counter. "Three sugars?"

Ruby winked. "I know what you like."

"Thanks, Ruby." Andrew took a long sip, then jerked a thumb in Sophie's direction. "I tried to tell this one we're capable of handling anything that comes our way today, but she showed up anyway."

"You know I trust both of you implicitly. I'm just here, well, because I want to be." Sophie lifted one shoulder, then let it drop. "Besides, my apartment is just upstairs."

"Excuses, excuses." The smile on Ruby's full lips took any sting out of the words. "Fess up. You wanted to see us."

Sophie rolled her eyes, but knew there was truth in Ruby's offhand comment. She loved spending time with Ruby and Andrew.

"I'm going to take my coffee with me to the back room. We have quite a few items needing sales tags." Andrew shifted his gaze to Ruby and gestured with his hand holding the cup. "Yell if you need me."

Just before he stepped out of sight, Andrew turned and pinned Sophie with a stern gaze, a look spoiled when his glasses slipped down. "Have fun today. That's an order."

Chuckling, Sophie gave a mock salute. "Yes, sir."

Sophie couldn't believe the change in Andrew. When he'd started working for her last year, he'd been oh-so-serious. She liked that he now felt comfortable enough to crack jokes and give her grief.

"Andrew fits right in." Lifting the cup, Sophie took a sip of the mocha latte Ruby had brought her. "Thank you for this. It's yummy."

"You're very welcome." Ruby sat on a stool at the counter and studied Sophie. "I'm glad you decided to take some time off."

"Me, too." Sophie smiled. "Volunteering refills my bucket."

Ruby swiveled on her stool to fully face Sophie. "A Chautauqua is your kind of thing."

"Yes, it is."

Chautauqua, an adult education and social movement popular in the late nineteenth and early twentieth centuries, had recently experienced a resurgence. GraceTown had chosen to re-create performances from 1916 and had encouraged those in the community to attend dressed in period garb.

When Sophie had been asked to volunteer, she'd eagerly accepted and had persuaded her boyfriend, Dylan Connors, to sign up with her.

"You'll have a blast." Ruby's gaze returned to Sophie's blue sailor dress. "That dress is absolutely adorable on you."

"I love it." As Sophie gave a little twirl, she couldn't stop herself from casting one last glance in the mirror. The red necktie, a last-minute addition to the sailor dress, added a nice pop of color. "I can't wait to get to the fairgrounds and see what everyone else is wearing."

Ruby inclined her head. "I didn't realize women wore such cute clothes in 1916. For some reason I had the impression you couldn't show ankles until the 1920s."

"That was how it was in the early 1900s, but by 1916, skirts were on the rise," Sophie assured Ruby.

"Your knowledge of history is only one of the reasons Timeless Treasures is so successful." Ruby glanced at the shiny hardwood floor, then sniffed. "Not only do we have all sorts of fabulous antiques, instead of mold and dust, the place is spotless and smells terrific."

Sophie puffed up with pride.

Five years ago, after purchasing the store in GraceTown's historic district from money bequeathed to her in her grandmother's will, Sophie had gone into research mode, determined to make the store a success.

When she'd come across studies showing that smells not only influenced people's emotions but their spending, she'd begun infusing a simple orange scent into her store. That was only one of many changes she'd implemented.

While her parents worried about all the hours she put in at Timeless Treasures, Sophie loved every aspect of the antique store business.

Though she'd enjoyed her work as an archivist at Collister College, dealing with antiques day in and day out was a dream come true. She couldn't imagine anything better than owning a business that dealt in objects connected to the lives of people in the past.

The vintage grandmother's clock chimed the hour, and Sophie realized with a start that it was time to open the shop. "I'll unlock the door."

"I can do it." Ruby stood.

"I got it." Sophie waved her friend back down, reaching the front door just as the clock stopped chiming.

With quick practiced moves, Sophie flipped the sign from Closed to Open and pulled up the shade, signaling that Timeless Treasures was open for business.

She turned back to Ruby. "Since my shift at the fairgrounds doesn't begin until noon, I thought I'd start going through the steamer trunk from the Wexman estate."

"You don't need to do that now," Ruby protested. "You're off duty, remember?"

"I've been looking forward to going through the trunk and the boxes since they were delivered." Sophie offered a happy sigh. "Every time I see an item from the past, I'm transported back to that time. I love getting these glimpses into other people's lives."

"It's kind of ironic, really."

Sophie gazed curiously at Ruby, not following. "What is?"

"The fact that überorganized, take-charge, get-everything-done Sophie gravitates to this kind of fantasy."

"I don't—"

"Just keep in mind that even better than catching glimpses into someone else's life is living your own." Ruby's expression turned serious. "You do too much for others and not enough for yourself."

Sophie was spared the need to respond when the phone in her pocket buzzed. She immediately snatched it up. Even though it had been two years since her father's stroke, any unexpected call sent her heart into overdrive. "This is Sophie."

"Soph, it's Dylan."

"Hey, you." She relaxed her death grip on the phone.

Though a call from Dylan was definitely unexpected, there was no cause for concern. Still, it was odd. In the two years they'd been dating, she could count on one hand the number of times he'd called her. Texting was his preferred method of communicating.

"About this volunteering gig…" Dylan paused. "Something has come up, and I won't be able to make it."

"Oh no." Concern filled Sophie's voice. She and Dylan had cleared their calendars so they could volunteer together at the fairgrounds. It had to be something serious for him to cancel at the last minute. "Is it your mom?"

For the past two weeks, Dylan's mother had been fighting a bad case of shingles.

"She's good. This has nothing to do with her."

"Are you—?"

He didn't give her a chance to finish.

"I'm fine. She's fine." He continued without pausing for breath. "Gage and Len are heading out to the lake today. Gage rented a boat for the weekend, and Len's parents are letting him use their cabin."

"But you—"

"Since I'm already off work until Monday, it seems meant to be." Dylan spoke quickly now. "You'll have fun listening to your history talks. I'll have fun at the lake. Win-win."

"We had plans." Sophie forced a light tone. "You agreed to volunteer."

"It's late notice. I get that. That's why I called instead of texting."

His breezy tone scraped against Sophie's nerves like a rusty blade.

Out of the corner of her eye, she saw Ruby cast her a curious glance.

"Dylan," Sophie mouthed back in answer.

With that one word, Ruby lost interest. Although Ruby was always pleasant to Dylan and never said anything against the man —okay, *rarely* said anything—it was clear her friend thought she could do better.

Lately, that same thought had begun to circle in Sophie's head. She refocused on her conversation with Dylan. "So, you called to let me know you aren't volunteering at all this weekend."

He hadn't mentioned the other days specifically, but Sophie could read between the lines.

"That's what I said." He sounded surprised. "Weren't you listening?"

"Just wanted to clarify." Sophie kept the irritation from her voice. At least she tried to. Didn't Dylan realize he wasn't just bailing on volunteering, he was bailing on her? "If you haven't already done it, I suggest you call Alcidean and let her know of your change in plans."

Dylan hesitated. "I thought you could do that."

Though Sophie liked Alcidean, the volunteer coordinator could be a hard-ass, which was likely the reason Dylan wanted Sophie to break the news to her.

"I'll give you her number." Sophie rattled it off. "Have fun this weekend."

She was on the verge of ending the call when he said her name in that deep, husky tone that had once turned her insides to mush.

"I realize this is a long shot, but I wish you'd consider coming with me. Gage's and Len's girlfriends will be there." His tone turned almost pleading. "You work all the time, Soph. Would it be so bad to do something just for fun? Just for us?"

For a second, Sophie was tempted. Dylan had a point. She'd put in a lot of hours at the store this past month, so they hadn't seen much of each other. That's why she'd been looking forward to spending this weekend with him.

"I'd love to, Dylan, I really would." Her voice held true regret. "But I promised to help at the fairgrounds."

When the call ended, Sophie leaned back against the counter.

"Let me guess." Ruby brought a perfectly manicured finger to her lips. "He's not coming."

Sophie waved an airy hand. "Something came up."

"You're not surprised he's not coming."

Sophie wanted to deny it, started to deny it, then shrugged instead. "I'll probably have more fun without him. Dylan isn't really into historical stuff."

Ruby's expression turned thoughtful. "When you're not surprised that your boyfriend bails on you and you really don't care, that's an indication you're ready to be done dating."

"You know me, Ruby. I'm not the type of woman who needs to be attached at the hip with someone just because we're in a relationship." Sophie could have cheered when her voice came out casual and offhand, just as she'd intended.

"I'm not saying you have to be attached at the hip. I'm saying you should be able to count on your partner to show up for you." Ruby paused and appeared to choose her next words carefully. "Dylan knows how much you're looking forward to this weekend."

"We have different interests. I like history stuff. He likes sports. It's okay to have separate interests." Though she believed what she was saying, Sophie couldn't stop the wave of sadness.

"Okay, sure. I get that. But do you have any of the same interests? Wouldn't it be nice to have a partner you could actually share things with?"

Sophie thought of her parents, how they loved to cook together and had a shared passion for old movies.

"It would be nice," Sophie agreed, "but I'm not sure it's an absolute necessity. Besides, it's normal for romance in a relationship to fade as time goes on."

"It's been two years, not twenty. Besides, look at your parents. They're still thoughtful and romantic with each other."

"Yes," Sophie agreed. "Yes, they are." Ready to change the subject, she gestured toward the boxes at the end of the counter. "Enough talk about Dylan. I've got a few minutes before I need to leave for the fairgrounds. I can't wait a second longer to dig into the stuff from the Wexman estate and see what I bought."

"You were just at the auction last weekend." Ruby rose with an easy grace Sophie envied. "Surely you can't have already forgotten what you purchased."

"I'm honestly not sure what's in the boxes and trunk," Sophie admitted. "They came up at the end of a very long day when most of the serious bidders had left. No one remaining was particularly interested in bidding on them. I did it because I figured there's bound to be one or two things inside worth the price I paid. And this beauty..."

Leaning over, Sophie ran her hand along the rough and scarred, still-beautiful wood of the camelback top. "This steamer trunk was likely built between 1910 and 1920 and is a highly desirable piece. I sold a similar one last month for over $450. It wasn't in as good a shape as this one."

"You got a good deal."

"I got lucky." Sophie smiled. "You and I both know a good deal at an estate auction often depends on the size of the crowd and who is bidding."

She and Ruby started with the boxes. From the first box, they set aside a sunburst clock and a pair of gold-rimmed martini glasses. In the second, they discovered numerous pieces of costume jewelry that Sophie knew from past experience would sell quickly.

"Now, for the pièce de résistance." Crouching down, Sophie opened the trunk, surprised to find women's clothing from the early years of the twentieth century on top. She pulled out a spring dress covered in yellow flowers. "This is adorable. I love the way it narrows at the bottom, almost like a pencil skirt."

Ruby studied it. "With your dark hair, the dress is perfect for your coloring. It even looks like it might be your size."

Folding it carefully, Sophie set it and another dress in emerald green aside before lifting out a cream satin christening dress with scalloped lace trim.

Out of nowhere, an image of a baby with a swath of dark hair, bright blue eyes and a gummy smile flashed. An unexpected surge of longing had Sophie wanting to clasp the whisper-soft fabric tight against her chest. Instead, she refolded the gown and gently laid it atop the dresses.

A floral hatbox came next. But when Sophie opened the lid, she didn't find a hat. Instead, the box was filled with dozens and dozens of black-and-white family photographs from the early to mid-twentieth century.

Ruby picked up a few, shrugged, then dropped them back inside. "Kind of sad to think no one in the family wanted these."

Sophie felt a pang in the area of her heart. She found it incredibly difficult to toss away *any* photographs, even those of people she didn't know, but especially photos like these, which she saw as mini historical documents.

"I love to study the people in these images and imagine what was happening in their lives when the photograph was taken." Sophie reluctantly placed a photo back in the hatbox. "I'll go through these later when I have more time."

"Lookee, lookee, what have we here?" Ruby held up a small velvet drawstring pouch and gave it a shake. "Want to guess what's inside?"

Sophie cocked her head and considered. "A coin, maybe? Or a special piece of jewelry?"

"You only get one guess."

"I'll go with jewelry."

"I say coin." Ruby pushed the pouch into Sophie's hand. "Let's see which of us is right."

Loosening the drawstring, Sophie let the contents spill out onto the counter.

Ruby cackled—there was no other word for the sound she made—as she scooped up the gold coin.

"I win. Though something tells me this isn't worth enough to buy coffee at Starbucks." Her friend's brows drew together. "Whoa, what's this? The coin is normal on one side, but the other..."

Ruby flipped the coin back and forth, gazing at one side, then the other.

Sophie's heart skipped a beat when she saw the engraving. She nipped the coin from her friend's fingers. "Let me see."

Ruby leaned over her shoulder. "What do you think?"

"This isn't simply any coin." Sophie couldn't stop the smile that blossomed on her lips, or the heartfelt sigh that followed. "This is a love token."

"A what?" Ruby's eyes widened, then suspicion replaced the puzzlement. "Are you making that up?"

Sophie laughed and shook her head. "Love tokens were

extremely popular up until the early twentieth century. Coins were sanded, usually only on one side, and then hand-engraved with words, images or initials. This love token has both words and some nicely carved intricate vines."

Interest sparked in Ruby's eyes. "What does it say?"

"'Love Be Yours, Love Be Mine,'" Sophie read, then showed Ruby the flowery script on the back of the coin. "That is so incredibly sweet."

"There's the romantic in you," Ruby teased.

Sophie lifted her chin. "What's wrong with wanting to find true love?"

"Nothing. Nothing at all. But if that's what you're looking for," Ruby slung an arm around Sophie's shoulders and gave a squeeze, "I'm telling you right now, you aren't going to find it with Dylan Connors."

Grab your copy now! Don't miss out on this heartwarming story that will keep you turning the page.

# ALSO BY CINDY KIRK

### *Good Hope Series*

The Good Hope series is a must-read for those who love stories that uplift and bring a smile to your face.

### *GraceTown Series*

Enchanting stories that are a perfect mixture of romance, friendship, and magical moments set in a community known for unexplainable happenings.

### *Hazel Green Series*

These heartwarming stories, set in the tight-knit community of Hazel Green, are sure to move you, uplift you, inspire and delight you. Enjoy uplifting romances that will keep you turning the page!

### *Holly Pointe Series*

Readers say "If you are looking for a festive, romantic read this Christmas, these are the books for you."

### *Jackson Hole Series*

Heartwarming and uplifting stories set in beautiful Jackson Hole, Wyoming.

### *Silver Creek Series*

Engaging and heartfelt romances centered around two powerful families whose fortunes were forged in the Colorado silver mines.

### **Sweet River Montana Series**

A community serving up a slice of small-town Montana life, where helping hands abound and people fall in love in the context of home and family.